# THE RETURN

# THE RETURN

## Barry Faville

Auckland
Oxford University Press
Melbourne   Oxford   New York   Toronto

*Oxford University Press*

OXFORD   NEW YORK   TORONTO
DELHI   BOMBAY   CALCUTTA   MADRAS   KARACHI
PETALING JAYA   SINGAPORE   HONG KONG   TOKYO
NAIROBI   DAR ES SALAAM   CAPE TOWN
MELBOURNE   AUCKLAND
and associated companies in
BEIRUT   BERLIN   IBADAN   NICOSIA

Oxford is a trade mark of Oxford University Press

First published 1987
Reprinted 1988
© Barry Faville 1987

ISBN 0 19 558166 0

Photoset in Bembo by Rennies Illustrations Ltd,
and printed in Hong Kong
Published by Oxford University Press
5 Ramsgate Street, Auckland, New Zealand

# CONTENTS

# CONTENTS

# I

# ARRIVAL

There was once a time when Wilkes Beach was a world of its own, remote from cities, and far enough even from the nearest town to make the journey between them, along a dusty, metalled snake of a road, a prospect to be reckoned with. You travelled there because you wanted to or needed to. Except in summer, when a handful of holidaymakers arrived to open their baches or pitch a tent, the tiny settlement was left to itself — a few hundred people clustered alongside a beach, overlooked by a range of bush-covered hills.

The casual motorists who manoeuvred their cars round the hairpin curves and blind corners cursed the hills for being there and abused the engineers who had surrendered to the valleys and ridges, going over and around them, and never through. Their children blinked at dusty greenery swaying by, slumped in misery as the metalled serpent wound on, endlessly twisting and dipping, and they dreamed of asphalt.

But those who lived at Wilkes Beach gave thanks for the hills and prayed that no man would ever covet the ground in which the trees and ferns grew like something left over from the beginning of time. From the ferment of rotting leaves and fronds the bush sprouted fresh, lusty and alive, and to Aaron Clark it looked just right.

His boat rocked quietly on the sea about a kilometre off the beach. The fishing had been good. The box at his feet was nearly half full of terakihi and snapper. He leaned back in the stern of the small boat, sucking at his pipe, putting off the moment when he would have to start the outboard motor. It was a warm, gentle evening with darkness melting over the hills.

Suddenly, far back in the dusk, a light flashed. More than a flash. A pillar of light slowly sank to the ground until it disappeared. He could see nothing more in the growing night.

Aaron Clark was seventy years old. He lived alone, his wife having died several years before. For some time he had been aware that he was of an age when people expected him to do foolish things. He had noticed that passers-by spoke to him more loudly, apparently believing that deafness was the natural companion of grey hair and a lined, wrinkled face. Neighbours inquired after his health more frequently and he knew that the day was not far off when some well trained brat of a child would help him step down from the pavement. He decided quickly that what he had seen should remain secret. Seeing strange lights in the bush would do nothing for his reputation. For all that, he took some rough sightings on the silhouettes of nearby peaks to mark the approximate spot where the light had shone.

The position Aaron marked in his mind was a small basin cradled in the hills. Near its centre lay a clearing which the bush had surrounded but never completely conquered. And now the bush trembled. Leaves on the crowded trees still cringed and arched back on themselves as the withering heat cooled rapidly in the night air. Moments before, a metal disc had skimmed over the treetops, looped gracefully in a wide arc,

8

and hovered over the waiting clearing. The night insects were suddenly quiet, like animals tuning to an earthquake. They sensed the energy of something like a huge bomb smothered at the precise moment of its explosion.

The craft hovered. A beam of faint blue light darted down and searched the ground. Satisfied with what it found, the disc descended then stopped about ten metres above the ground. From its base a column of white light shot down. The ground trembled and jerked and the soil began to crumble, as if some huge hammer were pounding it to dust. Then the craft inched towards the churned up earth.

The white light softened at the exact moment, as it happened, that Aaron Clark glanced up from below and wondered if his eyes were deceiving him. The craft touched the crumbled soil then slowly disappeared, like a huge crab sinking into sand. Only a thin antenna was left visible. For a few minutes rapid signals passed far, far away into the star-lit blackness. Then the antenna, too, slid out of sight.

Myra Gibbons walked in darkness to the small cemetery. Her feet knew the path intimately because Myra walked from her door to the headstones as though moving from one room of her house to another, and the front gates and fences she passed along the way were like pieces of furniture she had known for many years.

All the streets in Wilkes Beach ended by surrendering to nature. The main street was simply the final stretch of the main road from the nearest town, with a few houses on either side. It stopped when it reached the northern end of the beach. All other streets were arms that stretched briefly inland or to the beach, and they all ended in sand or at the bush line or the gates where Conrad Madsen's farm began. Church Street stopped at the bush. The small church, shared by all denominations, was opened only for monthly services and for occasional weddings and funerals. The cemetery alongside was enlarged when necessary by pushing back the scrub a few more metres. The headstones stood like proud statues among the long grass, with narrow pathways winding between them.

Myra Gibbons barely knew why she was walking to the headstones at this hour. On this particular evening the falling of darkness had unsettled her. She had moved around the living room of the small cottage she shared with her husband, touching ornaments and vases, patting cushions on the sofa and stroking the old wooden jewel box on the mantlepiece with the backs of her fingers, feeling the silky patina of its surface. Finally she had put on her overcoat and left the house.

'I'm going up the road, Frank,' she called to her husband.

'All right love, I'll see you later.'

Frank was tinkering with an engine in the cluttered shed that sprawled over an area larger than their cottage. He was accustomed to Myra's regular visits to the cemetery and gave little thought to the fact that this was the first time she had ever visited her family's graves after dark.

They stood darkly silhouetted alongside a worn path. Four headstones in a compact group. Thelma Sorensen, aged 38 years; Edward Sorensen, aged 42 years; Charles

Sorensen, aged 12 years; Jean Sorensen, aged 10 years. This was Myra's family, resting in peace, and each of them had the same year engraved in the stone: 1899. Within three months of each other, they had all died, vague blurs whom Myra could barely remember as living beings, let alone recall the shapes and lines of their faces. Yet they seemed to cling to the surviving daughter and sister from their graves with a bond of memory and affection that could never be broken, and which Myra could not resist. Even when she had gone as a bewildered five-year-old to live with relatives she never ceased fretting, and was at some kind of peace with herself only when she returned to Wilkes Beach more than twelve years later.

There she had met young Frank Gibbons, married him, and settled in the small cottage that was still their home. They had no children, for which Myra was glad. Although she had survived, she could never stop suspecting that the disease that had killed her family still lay hidden within her, ready to be passed on to later generations. Frank had reassured her. The death certificates had said 'cerebral haemorrhage' which, according to Frank, meant that something had popped in their heads and they had fallen asleep, just like that! No disease there, Frank had said. They hadn't even been sick! Everyone knew. Even old Doctor Scandlyn said so, and he had signed the death certificates.

Myra did not grieve at the headstones. She simply liked to sit and pass her hand over their surfaces and feel contented. To their credit, the people of Wilkes Beach accepted Myra's ways and protected her privacy. Any stranger commenting on the eccentric, grey-haired woman who sat among the graves for a few minutes almost every day was told quickly by the cold stares he received to mind his own business. For Myra was a kind, gentle woman, as spry and fit as a fantail and friend to everyone from the time she peered expectantly into their prams. If she felt impelled to visit her dead family, that was her concern, because she had known them for a brief enough time when they were alive.

But there was one part of Myra's ritual that was private. On this night, as usual, after she had walked home, Myra lifted the wooden jewel box from the mantlepiece. She carried it through to the table, raised the lid, then ran her fingers through the coloured pebbles that half filled the box. Within the confines of the wooden walls the stones rattled and clicked like deep-throated birds as their colours swirled under the light.

Myra smiled as she smoothed the cloth on the table, then emptied the box before her. She shaped the round, smooth stones into a mound and, with slow deliberate gestures, moved them one at a time to form a shape on the table cloth about the size of a large saucer. She studied each pebble carefully, as though completing a puzzle.

Then she placed her hands on either side of the stones and gently squeezed the coloured mosaic. The pebbles moved, nudging each other aside, easing into open spaces, jostling against a neighbour. Myra's hands shifted with them quietly guiding the colours as they twittered to each other. Like a living organism beneath a microscope, the edges never achieved a perfect circle. They bulged and shrank like something fluid, and the more they moved the brighter grew the gleam of concentration in Myra's eyes. At last one of the pebbles surrendered to the pressure around it and popped into the air.

The game was over. Myra returned the pebbles to the box. She had gathered them from the beach over many years, always seeking those of the right size, as near spherical as possible and always with a colour that was unlike any other she possessed. Although she still searched as she walked the beach at low tide, more than a year had passed since Myra had last found a stone that was honoured with a place in her wooden casket.

# II
# KARL

Mr Lockett was the headmaster of Wilkes Beach School, an old wooden building with a peaked roof, a long corridor down one side, and two classrooms. On the far side of the asphalt square that lay at the front entrance was a shelter shed, and beyond that two outdoor toilets, separated by fifty metres of lawn. The desks in the two classrooms were solid and immovable with lift-up lids and openings at the top for ink wells. Their working surfaces were shiny with age and engraved with initials that more than fifty years of regular sanding had failed to remove completely. It was an old school.

Mrs Lockett looked after the juniors in the smaller of the two classrooms. In the large room Mr Lockett taught the older pupils, who were divided into several classes. They ranged from eight to thirteen years old. Each class had only a handful of pupils but, as they were supposed to be doing different work, Mr Lockett was even busier than Mrs Lockett. Despite the endless demands made upon him as first one group, then another, called for help, he managed to keep his sense of humour and somehow look like a kindly uncle who lived this hectic existence because he enjoyed it. He had a round, smiling face and a waistline that was slowly spreading — something he claimed he could not account for, considering the distance he covered around the room each day.

An inspector from the Department of Education once asked him why he stayed at Wilkes Beach when he obviously had the experience and ability to win a position in a much larger school. Mr Lockett replied after considerable thought, 'Because I like the excitement.'

The inspector retreated into the folds of his double-breasted suit and said no more, though he wondered how any normal man could find Wilkes Beach remotely exciting. If he had inquired further he would have discovered that Mr Lockett's 'excitement' arose from the pleasure of watching his pupils grow up unaffected by the demands of their own age group, simply because there were rarely more than two or three who had been born in the same year. His pupils talked and behaved not as their friends did, but as their own personalities demanded, and his own daughter was a splendid example.

'Jonathan, Belinda, Susan and Paul,' said Mr Lockett one morning, as though he were about to list the books of the New Testament, 'today you will be five.'

'You're teasing us again,' said Susan.

'We will not be teased!' said Belinda.

'A new boy!' said Mr Lockett.

'How deliciously obvious!' exclaimed Belinda.

'That's no way to speak to your father,' said Mr Lockett mildly. 'Yes, at last we have a new pupil to swell the numbers of the senior class.'

He ran his fingers through his thinning hair as the four members of the senior class waited patiently. 'Now,' he continued, 'as Karl is new to Wilkes Beach, I don't want him sitting alone. Belinda, you will move

15

to the empty desk behind Susan and allow our new boy to sit next to Jonathan.'

Belinda swept her long hair over one eye. 'Goodbye Jonathan, I will never forget you!'

Jonathan had grown accustomed to Belinda and ignored her. 'When is he coming?' he asked.

'He won't be long,' said Mr Lockett. 'Now, I think you're supposed to be drawing a map of New Zealand.'

He hastened away to start another group on its morning tasks. Jonathan resumed work on his outline map of New Zealand, preparing himself to deal with the complexities of the Fiordland coast. A busy hum filled the room until about fifteen minutes later when a face appeared at the door. Mrs Lockett ushered in the new boy then departed quickly. Her pupils in the junior room were doing finger painting for the first time and she was well aware of what might happen if she left them alone for too long. The new boy looked around him curiously. His face was calm and expressionless, but very wary.

'This is Karl Smith,' announced Mr Lockett. He introduced the four older pupils, showed Karl Smith where he would be sitting, and glared at his daughter who was muttering rather loudly about being rejected, supplanted and unwanted. The other three grinned to themselves and settled back to work as Mr Lockett explained to Karl what he wanted him to do. Jonathan moved his pencil with some relief around the Southland coast, then prepared to sweep with more confidence up the eastern shores with a few broad strokes. Drawing the South Island was no problem once you had negotiated Fiordland.

16

In between finishing the coastline and getting ready to mark in the rivers, Jonathan took time to relax and glance around the room. It was always awkward to begin contact with someone new and the longer you left the opening remarks the more difficult it became. He let his eyes slide nonchalantly to Karl's desk and saw that he was working steadily. Noticing Karl's pale complexion, Jonathan was tempted to ask if he had been ill but thought better of it. If he had been sick he might not want to talk about it. Jonathan located the headwaters of the Clutha River in his atlas and tried to find the equivalent spot on his own map.

The colours of the atlas page merged, sitting like a garish blob in the pale blue of the surrounding sea and, as he idly ran his finger over the broad blue expanse, a thought that had been niggling the back of Jonathan's mind suddenly bit him. He pretended to glance out the window, but stared swiftly once more at Karl's face. The boy's eyes. Blond hair, fair skin and *brown* eyes? They should be blue shouldn't they? Perhaps he had suffered some illness which had whitened his hair and skin.

Mr Lockett bustled back from the other side of the room. 'Now Karl, let me see how you're getting on.' He scanned the page. 'I see Jonathan has been helping you. That's very good. Keep it up.' He darted down to the back of the room to investigate a loud conversation about a lost pen.

Jonathan looked at his neighbour's book. He had made nearly as much progress as Jonathan. 'Did you do this work in your last school?' he whispered.

Karl glanced sideways and gave a smile that could

have meant anything. Jonathan smiled back. His new neighbour was not the talkative type, he decided. He set about drawing the upper reaches of the Clutha River. He was still puzzled. He couldn't be sure, of course, but he felt certain that this boy Karl had never studied New Zealand before in his life. It was something to do with the way Karl's pencil moved across the page, as though he was tracing over an invisible line without thinking about what he was doing.

Jonathan looked more closely at Karl's map, trying to appear nonchalant, and noticed that his own very original version of the crooked inlets of the Fiordland coast appeared reproduced exactly on Karl's page. He had the weird sensation that somehow he had told Karl everything he had put on the paper. Jonathan carefully shielded his page with one arm, corrected the shape of Doubtful Sound, then watched Karl from the corner of his eye. Almost at once the new boy did the same correction.

Lunchtime in the playground. Almost everyone had finished eating except for the little people who, only a few weeks at school, were still seated munching sandwiches, having taken much longer than others to prise the lids off their lunch boxes or fight their way into paper bags. Some of the children were skipping, chanting rhythmically and monotonously, while another yelling gang was chasing a football.

'Shall we play touch football?' asked Susan.

'You may if you wish,' said Belinda. 'Personally, I'm beginning to find that game quite unbearable.'

'You always say that the day after someone's dumped you,' said Paul.

'Well, this time I mean it.'

'Don't glare at me,' said Paul. 'It was Susan who dumped you.'

'That's beside the point. There comes a time when you must put away childish things.'

Paul scratched his head, rather like raking a ginger haystack, and smiled.

'What are you grinning at?' snapped Belinda.

'You're talking like Myra Gibbons again.'

'Mrs Gibbons, I'll have you know, is a very refined lady.'

Jonathan rolled over on the ground where he had been lying. 'Why don't you two shut up?'

'Well, I'm going to play touch football,' said Susan, and she ran off.

'What are you so scratchy about Jonathan? You've been moping around all lunchtime.'

'Careful, he'll bite,' said Paul, prodding Jonathan gently with his foot.

'Get out of it!' growled Jonathan irritably. He went on more quietly, 'I don't know. I suppose it's that Karl Smith.'

'Oh, don't say you're pining for me Jonathan,' gushed Belinda. 'Do you miss me so much?' Then she noticed the look on Jonathan's face. 'What's the matter? You look as though you're really upset.'

Jonathan shrugged. 'It's hard to say. There's something strange about him, but I'm not sure what it is.' He was reluctant to tell them about what had happened with the maps. It sounded so silly and trivial when you thought about it, and could be easily explained as a coincidence, or just a plain case of Karl copying Jonathan's work when he wasn't looking.

'Do you reckon he's been sick?' said Paul. 'He looks very pale.'

'He's thin too,' said Belinda.

'What's puzzling me is where he's come from,' muttered Jonathan. 'I haven't seen any new families moving in, have you?'

'I saw your father with someone new yesterday afternoon,' said Paul.

'My father? He didn't tell me,' said Jonathan. 'Where was he?'

'Walking up to the house at the top of Church Street. You know, that old place up by the bush opposite the cemetery. The one they used for the Home Guard in the war. And he had a woman with him. I didn't see the new kid, but she could have been his mother.'

'How do you know? asked Belinda.

'Blonde hair — just like the new boy.'

Jonathan stretched out on his back and chewed a straw, playing for time. It was humiliating to find that someone knew more about the comings and goings of his father than he did himself.

'That's funny,' he said. 'Dad usually doesn't let that old place except sometimes in the holidays. People don't like it much. Too far away from the beach,' he added knowledgeably. 'Mind you, it's a good solid building, but it can get damp and dark up there under the trees.'

'Well, I wouldn't know about that,' said Paul. 'All I know is that I saw your dad with her.'

Jonathan's father was the grandson of the Wilkes who had first settled the lonely stretch of coast. He had come seeking gold, quickly discovered that he was looking in the wrong place, and instead had bought a large area of land fronting on to the beach and stretching a couple of kilometres inland. Wilkes Beach appeared on the map.

Over the years the Wilkes' land holdings had grown smaller as different parts were sold for houses and cottages and for the two farms in the district. But the family had held on to several properties which were rented to holidaymakers or to people who planned a permanent stay.

Jonathan's father was landlord to the Wilkes properties, run as a sideline from his small general store — the only one in the village. It stocked everything from dish cloths to horse shoes, provided you knew where to look. So if anyone was going to rent a house at Wilkes Beach it was logical to guess that Jonathan's father would be involved.

'We could always ask Karl,' said Paul.

'Ask him what?' said Belinda.

'Where he comes from.'

There was a long silence. Finally Jonathan said, 'Let's wait and see. I'll ask Dad tonight. If he's rented them a house he must know something about them.'

# III

# NEW TENANTS

Jonathan stood in the bathroom inspecting himself in the mirror: Tall for his age, well-shaped nose, slightly turned up at the end, high cheekbones (like his mother), thick eyebrows (like his father), hair hanging casually over his forehead. Definitely handsome, there was no doubt about it.

'Jonathan, have you combed your hair and washed your hands? I'm still waiting for that table to be set.'

Jonathan hastily turned on the tap. 'Coming,' he said.

The Wilkes household was in the middle of its dinner-time routine. Mrs Wilkes was striding around the kitchen, mostly humming to herself but occasionally directing activities in the rest of the house. Mr Wilkes was listening to the evening radio news. Mary Wilkes, aged three, was trying to stop him, creeping up behind his chair, reaching up and pulling his hair, then running away. She thought she was very funny.

Jonathan emerged and began setting the table.

'I'm about to dish!' called Mrs Wilkes.

'Do we need pudding spoons?' asked Jonathan.

'Mary, go and wash your hands and leave my hair alone,' said Mr Wilkes.

'You're a pain, Mary,' said Jonathan.

'Stop bickering, you two,' said Mrs Wilkes. 'No.'

'What?'

'No, we don't need pudding spoons. Who wants gravy?'

'Yes please,' said Jonathan, 'but only on my meat.'

'I want peanut butter on mine.' said Mary.

'Don't be silly,' said Mr Wilkes.

'I'm about to dish,' said Mrs Wilkes. 'Do you want gravy, Jonathan?'

'Yes please,' said Jonathan, 'but only on my meat.'

'I'm going to wash my hands,' said Mary.

'I'm dishing,' said Mrs Wilkes.

Mrs Wilkes was a very good cook but she wrote songs in her spare time (and had sold several), and she liked to try out tunes in her head as she worked in the kitchen. Jonathan had finished his meal except for his green beans (which were covered with gravy) when he remembered.

'Dad, Paul said he saw you with someone up at the old place yesterday.'

'Which old place?'

'You know, the one up by the bush.'

'*That* old place,' said Mrs Wilkes. 'Don't forget your beans, Jonathan.'

'I've finished mine,' said Mary.

'You didn't have any,' said her mother. 'You had carrot.'

'That's why I've finished them,' beamed Mary. 'I made a joke,' she said to her father.

'Dad!'

'What? Oh yes, I was up there with a new tenant.'

'What was she like?' asked Jonathan.

His father scratched an itchy spot in his beard. 'The

new tenant? Well, her name is Mrs Smith and she insisted on having the old house. Not that I mind. It's always been hard to get people into that place in summer, let alone this time of the year. No one wants to live up there among the trees — not enough sun.'

'Perhaps she wanted the low rent,' said Mrs Wilkes. 'What does she do, this Mrs Smith?'

'I'm not sure. All she said was, "This is the place we want. It's perfect".'

'I wonder if she's a war widow,' said Mrs Wilkes. 'Did she say anything about her husband?'

'No, but she asked if she could pay the rent monthly — it seemed she had money coming to her once a month.'

'Well, that's what you would expect if she had a war pension,' Mrs Wilkes remarked.

'What's a war widow?' Mary asked.

'It means a lady whose husband was killed in the war,' said Mr Wilkes.

'Like Paul's uncle,' said Jonathan.

'What were you in the war Daddy?' said Mary.

'I was up in the Pacific Islands.'

'You weren't killed were you?'

'No, I wasn't.'

'Dad,' said Jonathan impatiently, 'what was Mrs Smith like?'

'Who?'

'Mrs Smith! Remember?'

'Oh yes, strange looking lady. She has very blonde hair. You don't often see that in older people.'

'My hair is blonde,' said Mrs Wilkes.

24

'But hers is almost white,' said Mr Wilkes. 'And another thing — she has very dark eyes.'

'Did she have much furniture?'

'I didn't see any moving van. Of course, she won't need much. The place is quite well furnished already, and the room out the back is full of old furniture and odds and ends.'

'Well, I know most of my spare crockery and cutlery went up there when Conrad Madsen and his mates were using the house as the Home Guard Headquarters,' said Mrs Wilkes. 'From what I hear, they used to cook themselves some very elaborate suppers.'

'I'd forgotten about that,' said Mr Wilkes. 'We left all that gear up there didn't we?'

The Wilkes Beach Home Guard Unit had been formed in the early 1940s when someone decided that the Japanese Imperial Forces might invade the country via every available beach, no matter how isolated. The few men who formed the unit spent most of their time on duty digging small slit trenches and foxholes on the slopes of the hills at the northern end of the beach. They were very glad when the threat of invasion proved to be imaginary and they could go back to digging their gardens.

'Mrs Smith has a son,' said Jonathan. 'He sits next to me at school and he's got blond hair as well.'

'Well, wherever they come from it will be nice to have some new faces around the place,' said Mrs Wilkes.

In the house at the top of Church Street, Jonathan's new classmate, Karl, had not yet begun his evening meal. As Jonathan had done earlier, he was standing in the bathroom at the basin.

With one hand he extended the upper and lower eyelids of his left eye and at the same time stared hard at his nose. As tears trickled from the eye he used a finger of his free hand to slide a large contact lens over its surface. The lens dropped into his waiting palm. He blinked rapidly to relieve the discomfort and then removed the lens from his right eye. The only thing worse than taking them out was putting them in. He placed them in a small plastic capsule — two oval lenses tinted a rich brown in the middle, shading to white on the rims. They looked more like transparent glass eyes than real contact lenses.

Karl placed the capsule in the bathroom cupboard and looked at himself in the mirror set into the cabinet's door. The eyes that looked back at him seemed to have grown larger. They were blue, the pale blue of the sky near the horizon, with an abrupt deepening of the colour at the centre of each eye.

Karl looked forward to this time. For him the end of the day and the coming of the night was a moment of relief because it marked the sinking of the sun. The blazing ball of light that could wrench his head into waves of pain had disappeared for another few hours and he could be himself again, as far as that was possible in this place.

Throughout the house the lights were dim. Each shade was fitted with a cap of dark plastic. The light from the bulb was filtered to a soft yellow glow, like the dying flicker of a torch when the batteries are low. The whole house was faintly lit by a kind of twilight.

Karl walked through to the dining room and sat at the table. Mrs Smith looked at him. Her eyes were the same colour as his.

'Have you left the capsule in the correct place?' she said.

'Of course. Why do you ask?'

'I've told you before,' said Mrs Smith. 'We must be ready to put the lenses back at a moment's notice. We can never know who might call. We would not have much warning.'

Like the boy, Mrs Smith resembled any other person except for her pale blue eyes and the unusually white skin that belonged in the shade. Yet, as they ate, they moved with a kind of care and grace that seemed practised. It was barely noticeable, but the way they moved their knives and forks or lifted a cup suggested they were taking care to avoid a mistake. Even as they faced each other across the table they seemed aloof and formal, with no happy chatter or relaxed laughter. They were like wary forest animals, always listening for a stick breaking far off or the beat of hawk wings high up in the air.

Karl looked at Mrs Smith's face. Her hair was tied behind and pulled back so that her skin seemed tightened over her cheek bones.

'Do you like my hair style?' she said. 'I copied it from a magazine.'

'I was wondering if our hair would change.'

'Why would that happen?'

'Will the heat of the sun make it grow darker?'

'I think not,' said Mrs Smith. 'Anyway, if it does it will happen so slowly that no one will notice.'

'People at the school have noticed my hair and my

eyes,' said Karl. He smiled. 'The boy I have been seated next to could hardly stop looking at me, though he tried hard not to let me see he was interested.'

Mrs Smith looked at him sharply. 'You have done nothing to draw attention to yourself?'

'Of course not,' said Karl. 'Not that he would notice anyway.'

'What do you mean?'

'I had to read him so that I could do the work,' replied Karl.

'I didn't realize how hard it would be to use a pencil. My hand muscles are still aching. I made it look as though I knew the work already. He was thinking about me, but he was just curious. He will never guess.'

Mrs Smith's face tightened. 'You must take care,' she said. 'One slip will be enough, and for all we know this boy might be one of those we are looking for. You might think he doesn't know what you are doing through him, but if he is a target you could well trigger an awareness in him.'

'But I thought that was our intention.'

'Yes, that is true,' sighed Mrs Smith. 'I suppose I'm being cautious. But when the moment comes — if it comes — I would like the evidence to come from a carefully controlled experiment, not just some idle fun.'

At that moment a high-pitched hum filled the room. A small metal box perched on a ledge above the door seemed to have come alive. Covering her eyes with one hand, Mrs Smith reached up and twisted the shield from the light before darting from the room after Karl. In less than a minute they had returned, their eyes now a deep brown.

The sudden blazing of light against the windows startled Myra Gibbons. She was even amazed to find herself in the driveway of the old house, walking up the gravelled drive, instead of retracing her steps down the footpath from the cemetery to her home. But then, she could not really understand why yet again she was visiting the headstones in the evening. She had felt impelled to go. Then, as she walked back past the church when her visit was over, her feet had seemed to walk slowly of their own will through the gate on the other side of the road.

When Mrs Smith opened the front door she saw standing on the edge of the circle of light a bewildered elderly woman whose grey hair seemed to sit like a glowing bonnet above her face. Mrs Smith was surprised and had to think consciously of what she should say. She was trained to respond to what was said to her, but she found no clue in the woman's face as to why she was there or what she wanted.

'Can I help you?' Mrs Smith asked.

Myra walked closer until she stood just below the step, but she still said nothing.

'Are you lost perhaps?' said Mrs Smith.

'This was the place.'

'I am sorry, I do not understand.'

Myra blinked and seemed to be awakening from some kind of trance. 'I beg your pardon,' she said, 'I am most dreadfully sorry. I cannot imagine what came over me.'

'That is quite all right.'

'I must have been dreaming,' said Myra. 'You see, I suddenly had the strangest feeling that something was calling me from deep inside the house, something

I had forgotten a long time ago, and I could not stop myself from walking closer. Then there were all the lights — lights everywhere. They gave me a shock.'

'I understand.'

'You must think me awfully silly. I'll go now. I'm very sorry to have troubled you.'

Myra turned, walked back down the drive, gently scrunching her feet in the gravel like a dignified bird, and disappeared into the darkness. But she still heard that faint voice like a fading echo calling her name, quietly and insistently, as though the house itself was trying to speak through bruised and battered lips.

As Mrs Smith closed the door she looked at Karl, who had been standing out of sight by the wall.

'There was nothing in her mind,' said Karl. 'Nothing except what she said aloud.'

Mrs Smith nodded. 'There was nothing else, but that does not tell us what brought her here. I wonder if this is the house where it happened. It is the correct location. I have checked that, but I cannot be certain that it is the same house. It doesn't seem old enough. She was a strange lady. There is probably nothing more to it than that — she is a strange old lady.'

Before locking the door, Mrs Smith walked swiftly around the grounds and looked down the road from the gate. A few minutes later the lights in the windows dimmed so that to the casual glance they were extinguished. Only someone staring intently would have been able to detect the pale glimmer from behind the curtains.

# IV

# DREAMS

Myra returned home that evening troubled and apprehensive. Frank, sitting in his armchair near the radio, noticed the change at once and, while he pretended to be dozing, watched her carefully. She went through her normal ritual, but tonight she was tense and preoccupied. The stones thudded from the box on to the tabletop in an untidy shower and one pebble tumbled to the floor where it lay forgotten. Myra's hands seemed unable to shepherd the stones into their usual pattern and even their colours looked sullen and dull. Finally she sat staring into the distance, her fingers idly jarring the stones one against the other, and more than a minute passed before she noticed that Frank had moved to sit opposite her across the table.

'What is it?' he said. 'Has something happened?'

'The house, Frank. The house opposite the church. I have the most terrible feeling that something is wrong with that house.'

Frank waited patiently. When Myra had something to tell him she always spoke like this, like small waves washing timidly up the beach with silences in between.

'I felt it as soon as I had left the graves tonight and was walking past the church.'

She traced one finger through the coloured pebbles,

31

parting them carefully, clearing a track upon the table cloth.

'I felt that house calling me. Does that sound strange?'

Frank shrugged and smiled.

'Of course it does,' said Myra. 'I know people think I am silly and eccentric but, like you, they put up with me. But you see, tonight was different. Tonight I was no longer — contented. There is something there that disturbs me.'

Frank put a hand over hers and gently squeezed the fluttering fingers. 'You mustn't be frightened.'

'I wasn't frightened,' said Myra slowly. 'I felt something drawing me to that house, and then the lights came on and I suddenly realized that I had walked up the drive without knowing it.'

'The lights came on?' said Frank. 'Is there someone in there? Dan Wilkes never rents that place at this time of the year. Are you sure there was someone inside?'

'A woman opened the door,' said Myra. 'Oh, I felt so foolish! I could not explain how I came to be there. What will she think?'

She began dropping the stones back into the box, brisk and business-like as though shaking herself free from something unpleasant. Frank watched her and made a mental note to somehow bring up the subject of the new tenant next time he spoke to Dan Wilkes. They were neighbours and saw each other often.

Frank Gibbons was a man often mistaken for something close to a simpleton. He seemed so commonplace, like a child's teddy bear to look at, with a portly body, stubby legs and a round face that always looked ready to break into a grin. He dealt in second-hand goods. Frank and his truck would disappear from Wilkes Beach for days at a time. The noisy old vehicle was always fully loaded both when it departed and when it returned — but never with the same goods — and in the transformation money must have somehow changed hands, because the back pocket of Frank's sagging trousers was always stuffed with banknotes. Frank was no simpleton. He was a shrewd man who kept his thoughts to himself and saw no need to waste his voice on anything that did not warrant it. When Frank spoke you knew either that he was interested or was about to settle a deal at a profit.

And now Frank was interested. He knew, as well as anyone, the house Myra had described. It was one of the oldest buildings in Wilkes Beach. Frank was more familiar with it than most because many years before he had helped build extensions, creating new rooms from old. He watched Myra dropping the last of the pebbles into the box and return it to the mantlepiece. When he walked to her and put his arm around her waist he could feel the tension in her body. As he gently kissed her cheek he could almost hear the echoes of the falling stones, clanging like metal, and it was as though his ears pricked like those of a strong but gentle animal who detects a twig snapping among the trees.

On that same night the same feeling was making Aaron Clark restless, as it had for several days. He could not forget that light he had seen far off in the bush. He had kept to his resolve and mentioned it to no one. But now, as he sat across the table from Conrad Madsen, he was wavering. Between them lay several stamp albums and, as they did once a week, they were examining, discussing and assessing postage stamps, collected over both their lifetimes. The living room of Conrad Madsen's farmhouse was like an album in itself. The walls were covered with framed photographs of people and places, some of his wife, children, and farm, but most of the vast family, living and dead, that he had left behind in Denmark when he was a youth.

Conrad spoke in a heavy, accented voice. He was a huge man with a powerful body and a mane of hair that was still blond, even though he was close to sixty years old. Aaron Clark never tired of watching his friend's short thick fingers manipulating the tiny tweezers among the stamps, lifting them like butterfly wings in hands that seemed born to grip the oar of a Viking ship.

He knew he could trust his old friend with any secret, but he was still not sure if he wanted even Conrad to know about what he had seen. Then Conrad Madsen said, 'What's on your mind Aaron?'

Aaron thought carefully for a moment. 'I was wondering about old age.'

'We are both old enough to think about that,' chuckled Conrad. 'What happened? Did you fall down maybe? Forget where you left your best socks? All those things happened to me last week.'

'I can vouch for that,' said Mrs Madsen from her armchair. 'And that was only last week.'

Conrad smiled. 'Hilda thinks I am starting to crumble.'

'You'll never crumble,' said Mrs Madsen. 'You'll just collapse one day like a building in an earthquake.'

Aaron made his decision. 'Well, I'll tell you,' he said. 'The fact is, I'm beginning to wonder whether I've started to see things.'

'See things?' said Mrs Madsen. 'You mean seeing things that aren't there? Well, if you start doing that, make sure you keep to elves or pixies, not like that great lump there.'

She nodded towards Conrad who grinned at Aaron. 'That was something that happened last week too. She won't believe me.'

'Believe what?' said Aaron.

'A few days ago I was coming in after dark. I'd been moving some sheep up to the back paddock. I turned to make sure I'd shut the gate and I saw a light up in the bush, way back in the hills. Just like a big torch that someone was shining under the trees.'

Aaron leant back in his chair, greatly relieved, but he kept his face calm and nonchalant. 'He could be right, you know. I saw a light of some kind when I was coming in from fishing last week.'

'Is that what you meant when you said you'd been seeing things? Well I never! I don't suppose it occurs to you two ageing gentlemen that you might have seen an ordinary little torch? People go tramping in the bush you know, or pig hunting.' Hilda got up, shaking her head, and went out to the kitchen to prepare supper.

Conrad lifted his eyes and stared at Aaron. 'That wasn't a little torch you saw was it?'

Aaron shook his head. 'And no one goes into that

35

bush tramping. There are no tracks in there. Not where I was looking.'

Conrad pretended to study a stamp closely for a moment, then glanced across the table. 'I tell you what. Maybe we should stay quiet about this and keep our eyes open. And we'll ask Frank Gibbons some time. He'll know if anything's happening up there. Frank knows everything.'

They returned to their stamps.

It was pure coincidence that the next strand in the strange web that spun itself at Wilkes Beach should also begin at Conrad Madsen's farm. The farm visit was an annual event in the life of Wilkes Beach School. Every year the older children walked a kilometre down the road to the farm to 'study' it, rather than roam, play and run over it, as they normally did. 'Learning How Our Neighbours Live' was part of the Social Studies course and, as Wilkes Beach lacked a ready supply of interesting, colourful neighbours such as freezing works, fire stations, fruit farms and airports, Conrad Madsen's farm had, over the years, become one of the most intensively studied pieces of land in the country.

By this time, several days after his arrival, Karl Smith had found his place and mingled naturally with the others. Jonathan noticed, though, that while he smiled and looked friendly he seemed at the same time to keep apart. He could not be persuaded to talk much about his past life. He told them that he and his mother had moved frequently and he had lived in various parts of the world. No, he could not remember much about those faraway places because he had been too young

36

at the time. Yes, he had been ill a couple of years before and often needed to rest. Karl seemed to live inside himself and not allow much to be seen.

Jonathan noticed, too, that Karl's arrival had subtly changed the way that the old group of four pupils behaved among themselves. A new syllable had destroyed the rhythm of Mr Lockett's familiar chant, 'Jonathan, Belinda, Susan and Paul.' Susan was in charge of drawing the map that was to be used on the farm visit. She supervised Jonathan and Paul as they drew in the main outlines, then, as the one with the neatest handwriting, she set about printing the names of landmarks and setting out the title. Belinda rummaged in the crayon box, borrowed from the junior room for the occasion, as she prepared to colour the bush and mountains.

Then Susan said, 'What will Karl do?'

'He'll have to be a spectator. He can spectate,' said Belinda. 'Is that the word?'

'I think Karl should do the bush,' said Susan.

'But I always do the bush,' said Belinda. 'I'm famous for my tree trunks.'

'Well, he's got to do something,' snapped Susan, 'and I don't see why you shouldn't have a change. You do the sea.'

'The sea? How boring! It's all blue.'

'You could slip in a few sea serpents,' said Jonathan.

'Great idea,' said Susan.

'Yes, I suppose I could,' Belinda muttered, 'a few writhing coils and bared teeth.'

She set to work quickly, but Jonathan noticed that her cheeks had reddened slightly and he realized that he might have contributed to hurting her feelings. All five of them settled back to work, but their chatter was subdued.

'What do you think of my bush?' said Karl a few minutes later. He had finished long before the others. His colouring was disastrous, spilling over edges and lying dark and heavy on the paper.

'That's fine,' said Susan, glancing at Belinda. 'It's — very good.'

Belinda drew another fang on a magnificent sea serpent that swirled from the ocean holding the map's compass rose in its mouth, a quivering fish impaled on the North point. Jonathan suddenly thought, he has no one to imitate. He's helpless. Then at once another idea struck him. Does he know what I'm thinking — now? Karl's face was blank.

Twelve of them walked to the farm — the five older pupils, together with the class below them. Mr Madsen stood by the front gate waiting for them, tall and solid like a log of seasoned wood.

'Most of you know me, and I certainly know all of you,' he said in a slow, deep voice. 'I remember you from the time you were babies, and it's amazing to see how you've grown.'

He let his eyes move in a leisurely way from face to face, and by the time he had finished there was not one of them who did not believe in some strange way that they all still belonged in pushchairs. Mr Madsen was an imposing man.

'There is one other thing,' he continued, 'and I want you to remember it. You must do as I say every moment you are here. It's the dogs, you see. Some dogs do not care for strangers. You are safe as long as you stay close to me, but if you wander away who knows what might happen?'

One or two of the younger children looked impressed, but Susan muttered, 'Does he mean Blue?'

'He means Blue,' whispered Paul. 'That's the only dog he owns.'

'Blue wouldn't do anything to you except lick your legs.'

Blue was a drooling-tongued, friendly old dog who was utterly harmless. When he was not plodding around the farm behind his master, Blue spent his days seeking out sunny corners where he could sleep undisturbed. The only animals on the farm to show the slightest concern about Blue's approach were day-old calves. By the time they were two days old they charged him on sight, if they could manage to run without falling over.

For all that, Mr Lockett's children always behaved themselves on the farm tour. They had seen it all before, of course, because they ranged all over the Madsen farm whenever they wanted. It was one of the quickest ways to get from the village to their favourite parts of the bush. But they looked at familiar sights through new eyes when Mr Madsen was in command. They tramped very carefully round the sheep yards, then over to the small shed where the handful of house cows were milked. They tried to jot down facts and figures as they walked, and struggled to fill in spaces on the map, with the large sheet of paper rolling and unrolling like something with a mind of its own.

Karl did not help. He walked a little apart, looking interested. But his face was taut and wary, like an explorer respecting the unknown. He did not seem to hear Belinda when she asked him to hold down a corner of the map. He concentrated on Mr Madsen, and what he had to say, like a devoted worshipper in a church.

'Here, I'll do it,' said Jonathan.

'Thanks. I hope he steps in a cowpat. He hasn't done a thing,' muttered Belinda.

'Perhaps it's new to him,' said Susan.

'So what!'

When he looked back later, Jonathan realized that the little flurry of irritation that had swirled among them at that moment was the real cause of what happened next. They were walking through the paddock where Sweetie lived. She was an elderly black and white Friesian cow who was named after her great love — sugar lumps. She had been reared by hand after her mother had died and she had grown up as the family pet. Now she was very old but she still lived in hope of receiving a lump of sugar from anyone who came near. Whenever someone walked through the house paddock she would follow a few steps behind, occasionally nudging at a pocket with her wet nose if she thought she would be rewarded.

Karl did not know this. He was lagging behind, gazing around, when he felt a bump on his back. Turning, he saw Sweetie's huge head and her slobbery, moist muzzle stretched out towards him. Karl screamed. He ran, and Sweetie lumbered after him, nudging at his swerving back. He ran and ran until he reached the gate and almost plunged through the rails before he scrambled and half fell over the top.

Jonathan and the others looked on, amazed. They all knew old Sweetie. She was just a friendly old cow, like an ancient cuddly toy. Then Jonathan saw Karl's white, strained face staring back through the rails of the gate and he could see the fear and terror in his eyes. He felt a sudden urge to run over and help him, but before he could move the awkward silence was broken by a loud yell of laughter.

'He's scared of a cow! He's frightened of old Sweetie!'

'Karl ran away from a cow!'

'Did you see him run?'

Everyone was laughing and Jonathan joined in. Joining in was something you did without thinking. So Jonathan laughed too.

Karl's fear slowly drained away and he became himself again. As the others walked over to him he made an effort to smile. Of all the laughing faces the one he looked at was Jonathan's, because Jonathan was thinking, 'That's something new you won't forget in a hurry!' And he turned away and did not notice Jonathan's face colour slightly as he instantly regretted his hidden meanness.

Mr Madsen leaned over the gate. 'Did the cow give you a fright lad? Don't you worry about it. When you get to know her you'll find she's as harmless as the dog.' He smiled and patted Karl on the head, but did not see the cold glitter in the boy's eyes.

That night Jonathan had the first of the strange dreams that he would never forget. He had been quieter than usual that evening. In fact his mother asked him if he was feeling sick. Jonathan was thinking about Karl Smith and the cow. He felt uncomfortable as he remembered the way they had laughed. But it was stupid thinking like that. Everyone would have forgotten about it by morning.

He went to bed early and was quickly asleep. The dream began like the beginning of a film in which he seemed to be watching himself as the hero. He was walking across a paddock — the one on the Madsen farm that ran up to the scrub fringing the bush. He often played there, sometimes alone, sometimes with friends. Today he was alone. The grass was dry and green and the cows walked munching with lowered heads, as though they were performing a slow, stately dance. After a few browsing steps they gently lifted their heads and gazed peacefully at nothing in particular.

Jonathan walked up the hill to the edge of the scrub and flopped down on the grass to rest. Lying on his side, he watched the cows feeding. He noticed one of the animals on the far side of the paddock turn to look at him. It stared. Slowly at first, it began to walk towards him. All at once the sun lost its warmth and Jonathan's skin tingled with cold. He rose slowly, trying to keep calm and relaxed as he walked towards the scrub. At the beginning of the track he looked back. The cow was halfway up the hill moving fast, tail stuck straight out behind, neck and head stretched foward.

Jonathan ran. He knew the tracks. He leapt over the fern, straight up the hill, then circled round going back the way he had come until he slipped into a grove of small trees. He lay flat on the ground and listened. Nothing. Everything quiet. That cow! It ran like a lion! He lay still panting while his breath returned.

Suddenly, a strange wet noise behind him! He jerked around. The cow's head was an arm's length away. Two black eyes glistened at him and the mouth chewed up and down on strings of saliva.

With a wail of fear, Jonathan crashed out through the fern and floundered up the hill. He ran and tripped, staggered up and ran again, his legs scratched and bleeding. As he fell once more he glanced back. Nothing following. He stood absolutely still. He was alone.

In the quiet where nothing moved, he had the strange feeling that the whole world was watching and seeing more than he could. He walked warily up the hill. At the top was a clearing. He crept through the fern and looked out. There was nothing to be seen. Above his head the sky was empty and hard.

Then over the brow of the hill the cow appeared. It stalked over the top. More than ever, the animal seemed to possess the soul of a hunting beast. With lowered head it paced forward, tail lashing from side to side. In his dream Jonathan stood waiting, wanting to scream and run, but unable to move. The black head came closer. Its round, rubbery cow's nose suddenly stretched showing yellow teeth in a wide, moist mouth, lunging towards him.

He woke, sweating, with the blankets twisted round him in a tangle. For several minutes he lay still panting. He drove away his fear. There was the mirror, over there the wardrobe door and the dressing table. The crickets were chirping outside in the night. He could hear the flop and swish of the breakers down on the beach. He was in his own room.

At school next day, while they were doing maths,

Karl leaned across to Jonathan. He whispered, 'What do you think would have happened if the cow had kept on coming? You know. Right at the end when it was stretching out to get you with its mouth open?'

Jonathan's fingers tightened on his pen and his mouth went dry. He turned his head slowly and his eyes widened.

'Think about it very carefully,' said Karl.

At that moment, in the busy hum of the room, in broad daylight with the bright sun pouring in the windows, Jonathan felt a stab of fright worse than anything he had experienced in the blackest hours of darkness.

Karl leaned over as though he were going to borrow a ruler. 'I know how you feel, don't I?' he said quietly. 'It happened to me yesterday, didn't it? But I won't laugh. Now, let's get on with our work, shall we?'

# V

# MESSAGES

In the house opposite the church, Mrs Smith carefully removed a cardboard box from a kitchen cupboard. To someone casually glancing in, it would seem like nothing more than a box that might contain old crockery or glasses. She carried the carton to the other end of the house to an unused bedroom. There she placed it carefully on a table and slowly lifted out a metal box. From this container she removed a gleaming cube inset with small dials and lights that glowed faintly when the power cell was switched on. It was a transmitter.

Mrs Smith placed a small disc in a slot at the base of the machine. The power surged with a soft hum and for five seconds a series of signals beamed upwards like a needle of sound into far space. The electronic coding of the message had taken three hours to complete and was incomprehensible to anyone without a matching receiver. The message began with an identification signal, then said: 'Both members of the contact expedition have settled themselves in the target location. The shuttle vehicle is completely concealed. Our base has been established in a dwelling on the perimeter of the settlement, adjacent to a large expanse of natural vegetation. The local population have given no sign of real suspicion and so far our imitation has been successful. There have been no difficulties with language. Our prepared speech patterns have proved wholly adequate. The accuracy of the information provided by the first expedition on these matters is so remarkable that it makes the loss of the records of the experiment itself doubly frustrating. If only they had not been destroyed, I am certain that our task would now be completed. As it is, we must proceed by pure intuition.

'We have encountered only one major practical problem, and that concerns the effects of the sun in this planetary system. Although our information on its heat has proved correct, the effect of its brightness has been underestimated, possibly because the first expedition was present during a seasonal phase different from this one. We have experienced discomfort and pain and our eye protection has had to be made much more intense. The deeper colour in our eye shields has been noticed by one or two local people, as it clashes strongly with our hair colouring. I do not regard this as a serious problem. People seem to think us strange at first, but there are so many unusual hair and skin colourings among them anyway that our own strangeness passes unnoticed after the first contact.

'There is one further matter which I feel I must place on record now. The boy, Garl, has in many ways proved to be as successful as we had hoped. I regarded it as a good omen that we were able to adopt a native name for him almost the same as his own. As we suspected he would, he has adapted himself to his surroundings very quickly. We are regarded quite naturally as mother and son. My concern is that his new environment might be affecting him.

'The strong sense of independence and pride that our mind probe detected in him could prove troublesome. He keeps to the rules that we have set up for our own protection and concealment, but from the way he speaks of the people he has come to know at his place of schooling I am beginning to suspect that he is capable of emotions and feelings that we thought had faded long ago in the evolution of our race. Garl has the better chance to locate a mind that deviates from the normal, but his over-confidence could be dangerous.

'I am especially concerned about his use of his mind. His thought control is, as we knew from the start, developed naturally to an astonishing degree. I cannot equal its range and power. But I am worried about his use of it. Last night I detected a powerful outward mind surge. It was not directed at me, but I could sense that he was communicating. Therefore it must have been received by someone in this community. If this other person in any way realized what was happening we could find suspicions roused against us very quickly.

'So far I have not questioned Garl on this matter. If he feels he is being spied on he could well be resentful and close himself off from me.

'In brief, several strong similarities in Garl's character to the normal behaviour and characteristics of the native people could possibly work against us, rather than in our favour. If there are further developments in this area I will report immediately. Visha, Commander.'

Visha sent the same message five times at ten-minute intervals. After the final transmission she replaced the transmitter in its container and returned it to the cupboard. She strolled outside, deep in thought, to sit on a bench in the deep shade of an old tangled grapevine that arched over a wooden arbour.

Seen in the half light she could have been an older Garl. Her blonde hair swept back from her forehead without a parting. Her face was pale and smooth, the skin devoid of the creases and faint contours that spring from a lifetime of laughter or frowning. It was a face that had never spoken and could not be read.

She wondered if despatching the message had been necessary, worth worrying about. Then she recalled what had happened last time. They must record everything, even if it seemed trivial, and this time the records must not be lost. If anything happened, at least the Rulers would know.

Should she speak to Garl? Better to take the risk and leave him and see what he found. He had something in him that was beyond her. She must hope that he would confide in her if he needed to. She had often asked herself why they had sent him with her. They knew that he was different. But she was becoming aware that that was the very reason he was here.

Visha took from her pocket a small box and removed from it a globe composed of many small crystal balls the size of marbles. She held the sphere in her hand and passed her fingers over the glassy knobbled surface, gazing into its transparency. And as she did so, the crystals slowly filled with colour — oranges, reds, blues, greens and yellows seeped into the sphere like an imprisoned rainbow. Then she made the colours move and swirl, swarming in currents from one side to the other as though they were dancing to her command.

For several minutes Visha let the colours dance, then

allowed them to slow and finally fade. What lies within us that makes this silly toy such a comfort when we are far from home, Visha thought. Because it reminds us of home? But it was more than that. Visha sometimes believed it was all her people had left to them of a god. She had never forgotten the record left behind by the expedition to the nineteenth galaxy.

They had all died. She had always remembered. In the last words on the record log they said they were making the colours dance, and it gave them an extraordinary sense of peace and acceptance of what was to come. When the log was recovered many people were amused at what they heard, but Visha had asked herself at the time, 'Who knows more than someone about to die? And what can be more powerful than something that comforts the dying?'

Visha replaced the globe in its container and held it up on the tips of her fingers. These things were so common that children played with them to exercise their minds. And the Rulers wore a cluster of spheres hung around their necks. Perhaps she and her people had something born into them — a people born to make the colours dance. She recalled the words of one of the Rulers, chatting to her as he farewelled the tiny expedition before its departure for the Third Planet: 'When we conduct our little experiments around the universe, who knows what stray threads we weave into new minds without knowing what we have done?'

Visha tried to push the thought from her head and returned the small globe to her pocket. But a few minutes later she was again holding the marbled orb and moving colours back and forth in gentle swoops, in time to the commands that swayed through her mind.

Jonathan's father always knew when Frank Gibbons had something on his mind. He walked slowly round the store, humming softly to himself, closely examining anything that took his eye, and always taking care to buy something that Dan sensed Frank did not really need.

'I'll have a few handfuls of lead-head nails, Dan, if you don't mind.' Frank hovered while the nails were being weighed.

'Doing some roofing, Frank?'

'Some sheets of iron on the garage need replacing,' he said. Then he chuckled. 'It's been a while since I've done much roofing. I don't like the job much. You know, I think what puts me off was a job I helped on when I was a youngster, doing renovations on a house that had a roof as steep as a ski jump. I remember I nearly went over the edge, and I've never liked roofs much since then.'

'They can be dangerous, all right,' said Dan.

'As a matter fact, it was one of your places where that happened. The old house opposite the cemetery. You know the one I mean?'

'I ought to,' said Dan, smiling. 'It's the only one up there I own. I didn't know you worked on that place.'

'You were probably too young to remember,' said Frank. 'It was more than thirty years ago. The old place was ancient even then.'

'What did you do to it?'

'We extended out front. The old house was really

just a tiny cottage, and we turned that into a sort of service area out the back. You know, laundry, garage, garden shed, workshop. Then we built brand new living quarters on to the front.'

'To look at it you would never know it had been extended. Of course, carpenters knew what they were doing in those days,' said Dan with a grin. Suddenly his eyes brightened. 'I remember now. My father mentioned that place to me just before he died.'

'What did he say?'

'We were talking about the houses he owned around Wilkes Beach. He was recalling the ones the family had lived in and he mentioned the house up by the cemetery. He said it had always given him the shivers. Those were his exact words. "I never go near the place," he said. "Always gives me the shivers and always has".'

'Did he say why?'

'I asked him that. He said that none of the Wilkes family had ever lived in it. They'd always rented it to other people. Then he muttered something about the people who had once lived in that house and later died, and if I wanted to know more old Doctor Scandlyn could tell me.'

'Did you ask him?'

'No, why should I? I thought he meant that the house was too close to the graveyard for comfort.'

'Doctor Scandlyn died soon after your father, didn't he?'

'Within a few days of each other.'

'That's right, I remember now. It's a pity you never had a chance to take your father's advice. There might have been an interesting story there.'

51

'Well, if you're really interested Frank, I suppose you could chat to his daughter. He might have passed a few juicy stories on to her. If it comes to that, you could ask his grand-daughter.'

'Young Susan? Yes, I see her from time to time. She comes in to see Myra occasionally.'

Dan Wilkes laughed. 'The trouble with you Frank is that you haven't enough to keep you occupied.'

'You'd be surprised what I get up to in my spare time,' said Frank, as he prepared to leave. Then, as he was turning to go, he said, 'Well, I hope the new tenant in that old place doesn't get the shivers.'

'Mrs Smith? I hope not. It's not often I get a chance to earn some money from that house outside the summer holidays.'

'When did she arrive?'

'A couple of weeks ago,' said Dan. 'I've no idea where she came from. She just appeared out of nowhere with no car and not much luggage, wanting to rent something furnished for a couple of months. Strange looking woman.'

'Does she have any kids?'

'Just one, a boy about Jonathan's age. He looks just like his mother.'

'They're probably Scandinavian or something like that,' said Frank cheerfully. 'I'm told they have fair hair. Well, I must be off. Thanks for the nails. At least you don't need ration coupons for these. Won't it be great when we can buy all the butter we want? Anyone would think the war was still going.'

As he entered the money owing on the purchase in his account book, it suddenly occurred to Jonathan's father that he had not discovered what had been on

Frank's mind. But there had been no doubt from his cheerful manner as he left the store that Frank had somehow found out all he had wanted to know.

When school was over for the day, Jonathan did not linger as he usually did. He felt miserable and alone, brooding over what Karl had said to him. This boy, his own age, could plant in his mind any pictures he wished, and there was nothing Jonathan could do to prevent it. What other horrors could he conjure up to terrify him? His tormentor was free to do as he liked. He has power over me, thought Jonathan, and I can do nothing to fight back.

Should he tell someone? Who would believe him? Parents were all right for things they had experienced themselves, but they sometimes had difficulty believing things out of the ordinary.

He walked home and, after unpacking his schoolbag, wandered down to the end of the road, over the dunes, and on to the beach. The sand stretched in an arc for five kilometres to the south, losing itself in the haze of spray that always seemed to hang over the headland in the distance. Jonathan shared with many other children who lived at Wilkes Beach a fondness for simply walking on the sand. He had read a story once about a man who liked doing the same thing, but it was full of mournful descriptions about wailing seagulls and sorrowful waves and the sadness of this poor man who wandered the seashore. It was the most boring story Jonathan had ever read.

The truth was that, for him anyway, the beach was a place of endless interest where he never failed to revive, whatever his mood. The cries of the gulls were hard and sharp, sandhoppers leapt in showers from clumps of seaweed, the sea was like a gentle giant touching the shore, and day after day it left treasures lying in the sand: sticks, shells, stones, skeletons, all manner of things with names that sounded like the sibilant hiss of a dying wave.

Jonathan strode along the wet sand near the sea's edge, occasionally skipping a stone over a patch of flat water. Ahead of him he saw two small figures walking slowly through the soft sand near the dunes, stooped like witches in a fairy tale. As he came closer, they grew into Belinda and Susan, carefully picking their way through the dried seaweed and driftwood that lay like a fringe above the high tide mark. He meandered towards them, apparently walking aimlessly, until their paths crossed.

'What are you looking for?'

Susan glanced up. 'We saw you coming,' she said. 'Thought it was you.'

'What are you looking for?' said Jonathan once more.

'Stones,' said Belinda. 'Are you talking to us again?'

'What do you mean?'

'Well, you've been rather silent today haven't you? Not strong and silent, which I wouldn't mind so much — just silent.'

'Yes, I suppose so,' said Jonathan.

'What's up then?' asked Susan.

'Just something.'

'Ah!' Belinda exclaimed. 'Then there is something wrong! Told you so,' she said to Susan, prodding her in the ribs.

'Why are you collecting stones?'

'They're for Mrs Gibbons,' said Susan. 'They have

to be round and coloured, and they're for her collection.'

'She collects stones?'

'I've never seen them, but Belinda has.'

'It's true,' said Belinda. 'Some people collect shells, Mrs Gibbons collects stones. I saw them once. She keeps them in a box on the mantlepiece.'

'What for?' Jonathan asked.

'What do you mean, what for?' said Belinda.

'Why does she keep them in a box? I thought she would put them in a glass case or something.'

'I don't know. Who cares? She doesn't keep very many. Most of the ones we've taken her haven't been the right shape.'

'She probably plays marbles with them,' said Susan. 'Anyway, it's interesting looking for them for her. She's a nice old lady.'

'My ambition is to find the perfect stone, coloured ruby red,' said Belinda. Then she turned to Jonathan. 'So tell us what's been making you sad, poor Jonathan.'

'It's not funny,' said Jonathan.

'Who's being funny?'

'You are, and you'll think I'm being really stupid if I tell you.'

'I bet I can guess,' Susan said. 'Something to do with Karl?'

Jonathan was partly turned away from her so that she did not notice the sudden flush in his cheeks, but it would not have mattered if she had because she continued without a pause, 'You know, I'd almost forgotten, but something very strange happened this morning. Remember how we were copying from the blackboard? Well, I couldn't read what was at the

55

bottom of the board because Karl's head was in the way, so I thought to myself, "Move your head"!'

'You thought to youself?' said Belinda. 'Why didn't you say something?'

'I was going to, but I thought it first, the way you think something just before you say it.'

'What happened?' said Jonathan.

'Karl moved over. He didn't just lean over, he actually moved across in his seat. And do you know something else?' she said, looking at Jonathan.

'What?'

'You moved over as well.'

'Me?'

'Yes, you! You both did. It was as though you both heard me say something and you did as you were told.'

'I didn't hear you think anything,' said Belinda. 'Mind you, I have enough trouble listening to what people say, let alone what they think.'

Jonathan shrugged. 'Just a coincidence,' he said. 'Anyway, there's nothing the matter really. I got into some trouble last night, but it's all over. Come on, I'll help you look for stones.'

He hurried on ahead of them until he was out of earshot in case they questioned him further. How preposterous! He didn't remember Susan telling him to move. But what if she had? Perhaps he had thought he had really heard her voice. And could Susan hear *him*? Could Belinda?

Jonathan half turned until he could see the two girls. They were some distance away by now, strolling along taking no notice of him. He said to himself over and over again, 'There's a perfectly round ruby red stone two metres in front of you.' At the same time he imagined behind his eyes the stone his words described so crudely, peeping through soft grey sand, and his imagination made it almost glow red. Nothing happened. Susan and Belinda continued to stroll, though at one moment they turned sharply towards each other, like people who decide to speak at the same time.

Suddenly Jonathan felt as though a part of his mind had emptied, but in the strangest way. It seemed like standing in a huge, completely silent valley lined with echoes waiting to be disturbed. Or like creeping into an empty room, yet knowing that someone is there, because you can sense them. Then he knew abruptly, with complete certainty, that someone was listening to him. And Jonathan knew who the eavesdropper was, just as he knew what he would do next.

He continued to walk aimlessly, eyes on the sand at his feet, but at the same time he concentrated an image of Karl's face in his mind and thought the words, 'Come here,' with all the intensity he could muster. He was aware of his face muscles tensing, but he tried to keep his legs in a relaxed walk, as though they were remote and not part of him. Then he held the idea in his head, shutting out all sounds and fixing his gaze on a piece of driftwood a few metres in front of him.

For about two minutes nothing happened. Then Jonathan was suddenly aware of something approaching, an uncanny feeling like hearing far off footsteps whispering through undergrowth, growing louder yet somehow still soft and fuzzy, spreading through his head, a sound without any shape, with no beginning or end, pressing like a slowly clenching fist. He almost lost his own thought and Karl's image and fought to hold it. Then his mind was clear. In that same instant he found himself looking at the sand dunes as Karl's head appeared against the skyline.

Jonathan felt his skin tingle and the hairs on his head stir and prickle. He stared at Karl. The same thought struck them simultaneously. Jonathan stood astonished with his mouth hanging open and said to himself, 'I brought you here.' And Karl nodded, raised his hand in a kind of salute, then disappeared as suddenly and quietly as he had come.

'Jonathan!'

'Jonathan, are you deaf?'

He heard Susan and Belinda shouting to him from further down the beach. 'Sorry, I was dreaming. What did you say?'

They walked towards him. 'What's the matter? You looked as though you were in a trance,' said Belinda.

'I was thinking. Did you want something?'

'We wanted to know if you'd found anything.'

'No, sorry I haven't, and I've got to go now. I'll see you later, said Jonathan. He hurried off before they could ask more questions.

'There's something going on,' said Susan. 'That was Karl up there.'

'Where? I didn't see anyone,' said Belinda.

'Did you sort of — feel something strange a few minutes ago? In your head?'

'I felt nothing, but you did, didn't you? You stared at me all of a sudden.'

'It was the strangest sensation,' said Susan. 'Like people talking behind lots of closed doors, and all you can hear are vibrations.'

'Let's forget it,' said Belinda. 'I'm beginning to feel spiders crawling up my back. What'll we do with these stones? Shall we take them up to Mrs Gibbons now?'

'Myra can wait until tomorrow,' said Susan. 'We'll go to see her around afternoon tea time.'

That night Jonathan dreamed again, yet it wasn't a dream, because the moment it began he was somehow conscious of it happening as he slept. And he was aware of wisps of feathery sound filling his head with a whistling melody, and he knew that was wrong because true dreams are silent. The sound made him drowsy and relaxed, even while he slept.

He was high up in the air looking down on the beach. He was floating. Three tiny figures stood talking near the water's edge. They were Belinda, Susan and himself. He saw himself walk ahead of the others. Then he stopped, standing rigid. Another figure appeared, walking down the road. Karl. He walked quickly, almost running, then seemed to burst through the lupins at the top of the dunes. He waved briefly and turned, retracing his steps. Then suddenly he stopped and looked far up towards Jonathan, as though a film had stopped, frozen in its frame.

Slowly, like a child taking a hesitant first step, Karl smiled. Then once more, he waved.

Jonathan flexed his shoulder blades and instantly fell, soaring downwards, wheeling away to his right, then skimming the ground so swiftly that everything below was a blur of colour, swirling with sounds and echoes. Overjoyed, he swept up into the air again and gave a cry of relief, because he knew that everything was all right.

He woke to find his mother shaking him. 'That must have been a real nightmare. I could have sworn I heard a bird in here. All right now?'

Jonathan mumbled and smiled and was asleep again almost at once.

# VI

# DISCOVERIES

Across the road in his cottage, Frank was sitting in his armchair thinking to himself, 'Tomorrow I've got some finding out to do!'

A boy had brought Myra home that afternoon. Paul's mother had told him to walk home with Mrs Gibbons because she didn't seem herself. She had been hovering outside the house at the top of the road — 15 Church Street — and his mother had said that she looked like someone standing in a hospital waiting room.

'We live down the road a few houses away,' said Paul, 'and we often see Mrs Gibbons walking past, and lately she seems funny.'

'Do you think she's funny?'

'I didn't mean funny to laugh at,' said Paul solemnly.

'I know what you meant. It's all right.'

'I'll keep an eye on her whenever I can, if you like,' said Paul. 'I don't mind.'

'That's very good of you,' said Frank, 'and thank your mother for me won't you?'

Paul hesitated. 'Mr Gibbons — is something wrong?'

'What do you mean?'

'Well, I don't know. Over the past couple of weeks I've had a feeling that something odd is going on. Things aren't normal somehow.'

'Young people often let their imaginations run away with them, Paul.'

'Mr Lockett says that's what imaginations are for.'

Frank smiled, then laughed. 'I can't argue with that. I'll tell you something. I think you could be right. There's something here that wasn't around before. But don't you worry. You do what you said — you keep an eye on Myra for me, and we'll see what happens.'

Later, as dusk approached, Frank had wandered down to the beach to watch the fishing boats come in. There were never more than two or three of them. Frank enjoyed the quiet chatter among the onlookers and evening strollers as they craned over the boats to see the day's catch and pretended to help pull the boats up the beach. They would buy fish if they wanted them and disappear into the dusk at the same leisurely pace as they had arrived.

Frank was surprised to see the tall, solid Conrad Madsen standing near the water's edge watching a boat carefully riding the inshore waves.

'It's not often we see you down here in the evening, Conrad.'

'Hello Frank. No, I have little time for evening strolls, but Aaron promised me a snapper. That's him coming in.'

'Yes, I thought I saw him going out this morning.'

'It has been a nice day,' said Conrad, 'a very nice day.'

Conrad found small talk very tiring. The truth was, he was on the beach waiting for Aaron because the pair of them wanted to have a serious talk with Frank without his knowing it. The only place they knew of where they could be sure to bump into Frank without making a special visit was on the beach on an evening when fishing boats were coming home. Aaron had told Conrad to leave the talking to him, which Conrad was happy to do because he hadn't the faintest idea how they were going to bring up the subject of strange lights in the hills without sounding like characters from a comic strip. So he was relieved to see Aaron's boat grounding on the sand because it gave him something to do and to talk about.

After they had hauled up the boat in its cradle, dismounted the outboard motor and stowed all the loose gear, they stood together chatting about the fishing prospects for the rest of the week. The sun had sunk below the hills and the bush was darkening. Conrad waited patiently to hear how Aaron would subtly steer the conversation to the subject they really wanted to discuss. But Aaron had decided not to waste time.

'Frank, do you get up into the bush very often?'

'I've been round most of those hills up there. Not so much these days of course — I'm not as young as I was.'

'Have you been up by that middle peak?'

'Where?'

'Up there in that basin, just below the big hill in the middle.'

He pointed to the darker patch that was now almost indistinguishable from the rest of the bush with the night coming down.

'I have, as a matter of fact,' said Frank. 'A few years ago — about fifteen years ago to be exact — I had a good look around those hills.'

'What for?' Conrad asked.

'I was looking for gold.'

'Gold? No one ever found any gold in those hills,' said Aaron.

'I know they didn't, including me. So why are you two so interested all of a sudden that you have to arrange to meet me down here?'

'Arrange? What's this arrange?' spluttered Conrad. 'I told you I was meeting Aaron to get some fish.'

'Yes,' said Frank with a smile, 'for the first time in all the years I've known you. You never come down here at this time of the day. So come on, what do you two want from me?'

Conrad blew his nose and left the talking to Aaron.

'This is among the three of us,' said Aaron. 'Conrad knows already, but we thought you ought to know.'

'Don't worry Aaron, I can keep a secret.'

'At the time I swore I would never tell anyone, but — well, things have changed. A few weeks ago I was coming into shore one evening, about this time. I had a clear view of the valley and the sun had gone right down behind the hills. No sun — nothing to reflect from anything.'

'I'm with you,' said Frank.

'Well, I saw a column of light up in that basin. It seemed to come up right out of the ground. It lasted for a few seconds, then it was gone.'

'Is that all?'

'I saw it too from the farm,' said Conrad, 'just like Aaron. A column of light.'

Frank leaned back against the boat trailer. 'You know, what puzzles me is this. Why have you come straight out and told me? How do you know I won't laugh at you and pass the story around so that everyone else can have a good laugh too?'

'I have two reasons,' said Aaron. 'The first is that

I know you would never make fun of two old citizens like Conrad and me. You're too much of a gentleman.'

'Second reason?'

Conrad smiled knowingly. 'You have been nosing around asking questions, Frank. I talked to Dan Wilkes. He told me you were in his store trying to find out something. Only trouble was, he was not sure what you really wanted to know, but he said you went away happy.'

'That's true enough,' Frank chuckled. 'But what's that to do with lights in the bush?'

'Well Frank,' said Aaron, 'Conrad and I have come to the conclusion that something odd is going on around here.'

'You're the second person to say that to me today.'

'And we think you might feel the same way,' Aaron continued, 'so we thought a little more fuel to get your imagination burning might not be a bad thing.'

Frank looked at them like a wise old teddy bear. He grinned. 'I think you're right. There are little whispers all around.' His grin disappeared. 'And there's another thing. Something's happening, or someone's doing something to my Myra, and I don't like that.'

'Someone is harming her?' growled Conrad.

'No, not exactly, but something is upsetting her, pushing her off keel, if you see what I mean, and it's time to find out what it is.'

'In other words,' said Aaron, 'we have too many "somethings" floating around, and it's time we hooked a couple of them.'

'If you want to put it like that,' said Frank, 'but suppose you leave it with me for a couple of days.'

'You have some ideas?' Conrad asked.

'One or two. To start with, I'd like to look at that basin up in the hills.'

When they turned to look, the black patch had been swallowed by the darkness of the whole landscape.

'It's a long way to walk,' said Aaron.

'Not as far as you might think,' said Frank. 'Besides, I'm still pretty fit.'

'Would you like a couple of fish?'

'That's very kind of you Aaron, I'd be glad of them. Goodnight then, and thank you.'

He disappeared into the darkness, leaving Aaron and Conrad to saunter up the beach to where Conrad's car was parked.

'Do you think he is really worried about Myra?' Conrad said. 'She has always been, what is the word — eccentric?'

'That's what's interesting,' said Aaron thoughtfully. 'Frank is devoted to her and protects her like a guard dog. He might look as though he doesn't care much, but believe me he does, and if he says he's noticed something you can be sure it isn't just his imagination.'

'I suppose we must wait and then see,' said Conrad heavily.

'Something like that,' smiled Aaron.

Frank walked home quickly from the beach but did not go inside. He left his fish inside the gate then continued up past the Wilkes' house, across the main road and up Church Street, walking quietly and keeping to the shadows of the trees on the verge. Well before he reached the end of the street he slipped quietly through the front gate of a small cottage that he knew was empty, and out through the back gate.

The gate opened on to an area of untended grass used by campers in summer, and beyond it lay the bush. By circling around, Frank was able to reach the trees well to the right of the Smiths' house and approach it from the rear. He followed a faint path that wound right around behind the property. When he guessed he was at the rear of the building he began to edge forward through the undergrowth, pausing frequently to listen. Apart from the steady chirping of crickets he could hear nothing. He suddenly stopped. The Smiths' back fence lay a few metres ahead. He could see the house, silent and dark except for lights shining dimly through two windows.

He stepped forward very slowly, taking care not to disturb any leaves or dead twigs. He reached a spot just short of the fence and was about to take another pace when the lights abruptly shone at full power. Frank moved back, then sat down to watch. After about five minutes the lights dimmed again.

Well, thought Frank, so they guard themselves on all sides and they live in twilight like strange night birds. Perhaps they have something to hide, or are their eyes hurt by the light? Looking at the dim shape of the house blanketed in the shadow of the tall trees, he remembered his youth and the days he had spent helping erect the framework and slowly filling its spaces with boards. Fresh-sawn timber had a tang of its own. It smelled of eagerness and a new beginning. Even then, the bricks of the tiny old cottage from which the new house had sprung had been weathered, growing moss in shaded cracks and crevices.

But despite being dwarfed by the newer building, the old cottage still kept its hard, craggy shape. It jutted from the rear and Frank could make out its contours, clinging like an ancient rock to the ground it grew from. Whatever it is that draws her here lives in there, thought Frank. Among the old bricks. Stones encircle her whole life. Headstones in the graveyard. Coloured stones spread upon a table. Now something has awakened deep in the bricks and mortar and is slowly tapping at Myra's brain until it begins to bewilder and confuse her.

Frank knew he could never allow that to happen, because the tenderness and love he felt for her was strengthened by something he had come to sense only slowly as the years had passed — that Myra had suffered as no other human being had. It was as though a ghost lived deep within her, kept shut away all these years behind doors in her own mind. But now the doors were easing open. Vague shadows were beginning to eddy and stir, ruffling her gentleness and calm.

Frank felt all this, but his conscious thoughts were blunt and direct. It had begun with the arrival of the people in that house. That is why, by the time he had returned home and pondered a while in his armchair, he had made up his mind. Tomorrow would be for some finding out.

Very early the following morning Frank told Myra that he was off for a day's fishing, but he went nowhere near the sea. He followed the same route to the Smiths' house as he had the night before. After he entered the bush he again worked his way along towards the rear of the house, but this time he kept his eyes on the low-growing bushes, especially on the uphill side. He found what he was hoping for. About fifty metres short of the house he came upon a few broken branches, withered and wilted, but snapped from a small tree as though someone had grabbed them to steady himself as he walked downhill. Frank looked carefully up through the tangle of ferns and trees and could make out a less cluttered channel — not a track exactly, but a route where the going was less difficult.

He walked up this faint path and was rewarded yet again. A few metres uphill there had once been a damp spot where water had collected and created a saucer of mud. The mud had dried and hardened, preserving the footprint someone had made there. Frank stared up the forested slope. The direction he was heading pointed almost straight at the basin high up in the hills. The landmark on the mountain peak he had selected for himself was directly in front of him. He set off up the slope towards the basin, not attempting to follow any path or to look for signs that someone else had passed that way. He kept his eyes on his landmark on the horizon and surged upwards.

Frank was no bushman, though he had done his share of hunting and tramping and could find his way around. But there was no art or skill in the way he moved. He could have saved himself much effort by following the valley and crossing the ridge where the slope was less steep, but Frank had neither the time nor the inclination. He tramped steadily upwards towards his target, ploughing through the undergrowth like a tank, hauling himself upwards with branches and protruding roots, veering from his chosen path only when the trees were too tall or the slope too steep. Luckily, the undergrowth was fairly open, but for all that he was quickly festooned with leaves, twigs and clinging burrs. Springy branches whipped back in his face and a continual spray of small beetles and insects catapulted around him.

After a couple of hours, Frank was sweating mightily and his eyes were stinging from the salty perspiration .that oozed down his forehead. Then the ground began to level off. He hauled himself up into the lower branches of a tree and, from this vantage point, was relieved to see that he had reached the edge of the basin. He was not so pleased to see the size of the natural amphitheatre. It looked much smaller from the beach and he realized that to explore it thoroughly would take him well past nightfall. He would have to rely on luck and instinct.

He lined himself up on a tall tree directly opposite on the far side of the basin and set out. Because he was no longer tramping uphill, he found the going much easier. He looked from side to side as he walked through the bush, trying to find something that might cause a column of light. He had no idea what he might be looking for, unless it was a searchlight. His feet made little noise on the soft bed of humus that covered the forest floor. Only the swish of waist high ferns and the piping calls of alarmed birds revealed that he was walking steadily forward. The undergrowth stretched all around, dappled by sunlight streaming through the crowns of the tall trees. There was nothing strange or unusual to be seen. Everything that grew belonged there.

At last Frank reckoned that he was somewhere near the middle. He was beginning to feel despondent. He decided not to go right across the basin and was about to veer off to make a sweep to the right, when his eye was caught by what looked like a very sick tree. He could see its crown about twenty metres in front of him. Limp yellow leaves speckled the upper branches and, further down, the foliage was brown and dead. He pushed forward through the undergrowth and suddenly broke free into a small clearing.

He looked about him, amazed. The trees lining the clearing were all damaged on the side where they faced inwards. The tender ferns at ground level had shrivelled to skeletons, their remains looking like sticks and wires. The leaves remaining on the taller trees were limp and withered, as if a blow torch had scorched them, but they had not been burned by fire. There was no sign of ash. The leaves were dead, as though a disease had swept through them.

Before him lay an almost perfect circle about thirty metres across, as flat as a bowling green, but without a sign of vegetation. It looked like a perfectly tended garden, raked smooth, ready for seeds to be sown. He crouched and ran his fingers through the soil, to discover that it was not really soil at all. The dirt was granulated, formed into tiny smooth spheres, like chocolate-brown rice. He squeezed a grain between his thumb and forefinger. The tip of his finger turned white with the pressure before the grain exploded into dry dust and floated away in the breeze.

Frank walked forward a few steps and immediately sank to his ankles. He scurried backwards and sat down. What could have done this? Perhaps there was something down there. He reached forward and tried to dig a hole, but as fast as he scooped out the dirt grains, more flowed in to replace them with a sinister, whispering rustle. Frank's neck began to bristle and a tiny shiver pranced down his spine. He suddenly felt the silence. The birds were quiet. The breeze crackled the dead leaves in the tree above him, then the trunk creaked as it bent to a rising gust.

He had seen enough. He turned and walked back the way he had come, but this time marking his trail by breaking off small twigs and branches from the trees he passed. Something was down there, he was sure of that, and it must have arrived from above.

Walking home, Frank found himself hurrying as the houses of Wilkes Beach came into full view. He could see the doll figures of people slowly moving about. He suddenly felt hungry and realized that he had not eaten since he left home that morning. Now it was afternoon and his shadow jumped and darted ahead of him whenever the sun broke through the trees at his back. As he scrambled down the last slope he could see the roof of his own house, slowly disappearing from view the closer he came to level ground.

Myra would be there sitting at the table knitting or embroidering, as she usually did in the afternoon. He hurried, imagining for no reason that he could think of, that she might be gone, the cottage silent and empty. A scene from a film he had once watched came to mind, an image of an abandoned house with shutters banging and clapping against wooden walls. He almost laughed with relief as he walked up the familiar path of his own house and heard voices from inside.

Myra was sitting at the table with Belinda and Susan. They were nibbling chocolate biscuits, making them last. While Myra sipped tea, the two girls drank large glasses of orange drink.

'Hello Frank,' Myra said, 'you're back early. Look what Belinda and Susan have brought me.' The stones they had found on the beach lay on the table cloth, two of them separated from the others.

Belinda beamed. 'She's actually going to keep two of them.'

'We've found some good ones at last,' said Susan.

'I really must disappoint you when I refuse them,' said Myra. 'I'm so sorry, but you know how I feel. When it comes to stones, there is no room for second best. They must be perfect.'

'We don't mind,' said Belinda, 'do we Susan? We look upon it as one of life's challenges. Besides, most of the fun is in looking for them.'

'I'm glad you've had some success at last,' said Frank, slumping in his chair.

'You look tired, Frank.'

'I am a little.' He turned to the two girls. 'Tell me the news then. What's been happening to you two lately?'

'We've got a new boy at school,' said Susan.

'His name is Karl,' Belinda continued.

'Karl Smith.'

'He has very blond hair . . .'

'And he lives in that house at the top of Church Street opposite the cemetery — you know, the one with trees all round that Jonathan's dad owns.'

'I know the one you mean,' said Frank. He glanced at Myra. Her face showed no reaction, but he noticed that she had taken the two stones that lay apart on the table and was idly rolling them together.

Susan chattered on. 'You should know that house Mrs Gibbons. You used to live there.'

The stones rattled on the table. Myra's hand quickly covered them. Her face was pale. 'You're mistaken, Susan. I have never lived in that house.'

'But you must have. I read it in grandpa's diary, I'm sure I did, and I've always meant to ask you about it.' She was unaware of the tension that suddenly vibrated between Myra and Frank.

Belinda caught the look that passed between them and realized at once that somehow Susan had blundered over the invisible line that separates the affairs of adults from the activities of children. 'Perhaps you were thinking of someone else, Susan,' she said. 'Anyway, it's time we were going. Thank you very much for the afternoon tea Mrs . . . '

'Just a minute,' said Frank. 'Tell me more about grandpa's diary, Susan. Now, your grandfather was . . . '

'Doctor Scandlyn. You must remember him. He kept a diary with a list of the people he had visited. Just the names and addresses and the dates.' She looked at Frank, rather frightened as she too sensed the unease in the room. 'There's nothing wrong in looking at it. There are no medical notes or anything. Mum wouldn't let me look at anything like that.'

'Of course she wouldn't, my dear,' said Myra. She had recovered her poise and began to gather the glasses and plates from around the table. 'All the same, I'm quite sure I have never lived in that house. As a child I lived about a kilometre up the main road in an old house that burned down years ago.'

'Well, all I know,' said Susan firmly, 'is that I've

74

read a couple of entries which say, "Sorensen, 15 Church Street," and that's the one opposite the church isn't it? And Mum told me that your name was Myra Sorensen before you married Mr Gibbons.'

'That's certainly true,' said Myra.

'Do you recall the date?' asked Frank.

'There was more than one. I think it was 1893 or 1892, or something like that.'

'Why, that was before I was born,' said Myra. 'That settles that.'

'All the same,' said Frank quietly, 'that's the first I knew that your family had ever lived in that house. Did you know?'

'To tell you the truth, I didn't,' Myra said. 'Isn't that strange? I suppose my mother or father might have told me, but I was very young when they died. I could have forgotten, I suppose.'

'Of course you would have,' said Frank. 'No one can remember back that far. Well girls, I'm off to cook myself something to eat. I'm starving. I'll see you later.'

Belinda and Susan used Frank's departure to thank Myra and make their farewells. When they had gone Myra followed Frank to the kitchen and watched as he stood silently at the stove.

'Frank, did you really not know that my family once lived in that house?'

He shook his head. 'I never knew. It had been empty for years at the time I worked on it. But that was long after they died. I don't even remember you when you were young.'

'Nor I you,' Myra smiled. 'But I recall very little from that time. Just vague faces.' She moved to stand beside him, picking up a fork to prod at the sausages that were beginning to sizzle in the pan. 'Frank, you didn't go fishing today did you?'

'How do you know that?'

'You don't smell of the sea. I always smell the sea on you when you go fishing.'

Frank shook his head. 'No, I didn't go fishing.'

'Are you going to tell me where you went?'

He turned and looked into her anxious face. 'Not just yet. I've been exploring. I want to keep it to myself a while longer.'

'To give me a surprise?'

'That's right, a surprise. And don't look so worried. You always like my surprises. I've never let you down, have I?'

'Of course you haven't Frank. Not ever.'

Garl found the report in his desk when he was trying to open a drawer that was stuck. He tugged it free and found that a sheaf of papers had been jammed behind it, shoved in and forgotten. He smoothed the pages and read them with interest.

It was headed: 'Wilkes Beach Home Guard Unit — Ground Defences in Immediate Locality'. He skimmed through the numbered paragraphs, disciplined blocks of print marching for page after page, each one with no more than one idea. Their rigid organization and formal language were completely alien to the free ebb and flow of his own mind, yet as he read he was fascinated by the meticulous detail of the report. Its author was bringing order and form to a jumble of thoughts and information, shaping them to communicate with someone else.

The report described the progress in digging slit trenches around the hills overlooking the northern end of Wilkes Beach and went on to outline plans for preparing gun emplacements should they be needed. Garl's interest heightened as he looked at the map attached to the report. It showed the small settlement itself and a track winding around the coastline to the north of the beach. Black squares marked the foxholes that had been dug, while small circles showed the work that was planned. The report was signed, 'Conrad Madsen (Sergeant)'.

Garl placed some sheets of blank paper before him on the desk and picked up a pencil. To his eyes it was as crude and primitive as a flake of flint lying beside an ancient campfire. Yet as he turned it in his fingers he was struck by the notion that, although his mind could project thoughts, pictures and ideas like waves of sound and light, when it came to using this pencil his hand was like an awkward crab, scrabbling to clutch and manoeuvre the strange object. At school he needed fierce concentration to force his fingers to shape the letters and words and at the same time concentrate on distilling his thoughts into these strange, clumsy symbols.

Garl printed the first pages with meticulous care, setting down his message like a scribe recording on parchment the mysteries of ancient peoples, or a man squatting at a stone slab with a chisel engraving a true and accurate record for all time. He smiled at his fanciful notions and began his message for Jonathan. He was sure it would be needed sooner or later. He translated the instructions of the Rulers into the words and tones that came nearest to the spirit of his model.

## INSTRUCTIONS TO THE SECOND CLOSE CONTACT EXPEDITION TO THE THIRD PLANET, SOLAR SYSTEM M5429

1.  *Reasons for Initial Close Contact Phase.*

1.1 *You will know by now that the Rulers authorized the first close contact expedition to this planet almost sixty years ago. (We are using the time system of the planet itself throughout these instructions). This followed a long period of remote observation of the planet and its inhabitants during which the final stages of the evolution of the dominant species known as Man, or human beings, or homo sapiens, was watched and recorded.*

1.2 *You will also know the reason for the first expedition being authorized. Among the many higher life forms we had observed in the universe known to us, this species 'alone had evolved to a stage closely resembling the physical and mental characteristics of our own race. Put simply, they were more like us than any other species that we had encountered.*

1.3 *The reason for choosing this particular moment for close contact was our discovery of a remarkable surge in scientific knowledge of the human race, at least in some communities. Over a period of about a hundred years there appeared to be a sudden advance in what human beings were capable of achieving. We could also detect signs that, in what the planet's inhabitants call the twentieth century, there would be a further advance of immense proportions.*

1.4 *An important question was raised by these observations. Was this display of new knowledge a result of the race evolving in a way we did not suspect? Or was it the result of a slow, gradual process that had been going on for centuries, suddenly revealing itself in a spectacular display of new knowledge and technology?*

*1.5 One development in particular concerned us greatly — the sudden appearance of firearms and weapons of all sizes, of a destructive power that far outstripped those we had last observed. These had employed gunpowder and flint striking devices that, while effective, were primitive by comparison. The appearance of these new weapons was but one example of the advances that had been made. They also aroused fears about the state of mind of a race that could so eagerly invent and manufacture them.*

Garl read through what he had written so far, then put the papers aside. His hand was aching.

# VII

## MIND TALK

Jonathan found that he could speak a language he had never known existed. He discovered that he had walked to the edge of a realm where dreams made sense and thoughts became sentences with a grammar of their own. Walking on soft feet he could pad from his mind to another, and delicately nudge the thoughts of others as though they were balls of fur. But only if they were young, he discovered. His father and mother had seen too much and their lives were guided by what they saw behind them. But Mary still spoke to whatever she found in her head.

Jonathan knew about Geoffrey. Geoffrey was Mary's imaginary friend. He lived in a well-furnished room in Mary's mind and was very helpful and very tough. He never cleaned his teeth. He was known to turn on his light after he had gone to bed and read until the early hours of the morning. He scorned all root vegetables and even refused to eat raw carrot, regardless of the ill effects it would have on his eyesight and the curls in his hair.

Mary once claimed that Geoffrey had shattered seven eggs on Jonathan's head and would not hesitate to do so again if provoked. On one especially daring occasion he had even been prepared to release caterpillars in Mrs Wilkes' hair, and only earnest pleas from Mary had prevented him from carrying out his threat. Mrs Wilkes had been very grateful.

But Geoffrey as protector appeared less frequently than Geoffrey as the helper and adviser. Whenever Mary was involved in a difficult task, Geoffrey was never far away and Mary talked to him constantly. She would ask him what he thought she should do next. She commented on Geoffrey's own activities, correcting him when necessary. And she listened to him. Jonathan knew she listened to him because she was silent and because she looked at Geoffrey's face, staring at him somewhere behind her eyes.

On the evening after the dream of the bird, Jonathan watched Mary playing on the floor with her building blocks. A castle rose from the carpet with tall turrets and sturdy walls. Its construction had involved much discussion and chatter, but now it was complete, except that Mary had overlooked one red block which lay concealed behind a leg of the table.

Mary muttered happily, 'And I think it's the biggest castle I've ever builded, and I think we should leave it up all night. That's what I think.'

She stopped. On an impulse, Jonathan concentrated his thought, as he had on the beach the previous afternoon, and imagined it floating in an arc across the room.

'There is a block under the table.'

But the sentence was an image in his mind and he tensed imagined muscles in his brain to gently toss it from him. Mary was immediately puzzled and looked around her. To Jonathan's delight she quickly crawled across the floor and looked beneath the table. She clutched the missing block and was almost back to her castle before she suddenly paused and again looked about, this time suspiciously. She stared at Jonathan, but he had turned away and was pretending to read. When he glanced at her a moment later she was back in her own world discussing with herself the placing of the red block. She gave no sign of knowing that a Geoffrey-in-disguise had flitted in and out of her mind.

During dinner that evening Jonathan tested himself again. He noticed a dribble of gravy on Mary's chin. His mother and father were discussing something about the store and were paying no attention to either of their children. As he had done before, Jonathan concentrated his thoughts. He instructed Mary to wipe the gravy from her chin at once. His sister's hand went instantly to her chin and cleaned it. That could have been coincidence, Jonathan thought, watching her from the corner of his eye, but he almost grinned when he saw Mary dart a guilty glance at her mother. She had heard the reprimand and she looked in the direction from where rebukes concerning table manners often came. Again she was puzzled, this time to see her mother apparently unaware of anything wrong. And once more she looked suspiciously at Jonathan.

Then she stretched her hand across the table cloth towards her mother's arm and brushed it with her fingers. Jonathan felt a flush of shame in his face. Mary was seeking reassurance and her action confirmed what he had suddenly sensed — that she was vaguely frightened. She knew something unusual had happened. In the brightly lit room hovered something she had always thought lived in the darkness of deep cupboards or in the furthest corners of the night. It gave Jonathan an inkling of what power could mean, and at that moment it gave him no pleasure.

For Karl, on the other hand, the discovery of Jonathan's crude, forceful power was an occasion of excitement. But his admission of what he had found was almost like a confession of guilt. He began by approaching Visha and saying quietly, 'I think I have found him.'

'I knew you had found someone,' said Visha. 'You must have realized that I would hear you.'

'I would rather we spoke aloud,' said Garl.

They moved to sit opposite each other at the kitchen table. They had begun to converse in separate rooms using words that had no sound and had never been heard or spoken except in the strange realm that Jonathan had stumbled upon.

Visha was puzzled, though her blank face revealed nothing. 'This is unusual.'

'I cannot help it,' said Garl. 'I wanted to see you.'

'Why do you shuffle in your chair? You are confused. Why is that?'

Garl shook his head from side to side, and Visha was alarmed.

'I wanted to speak aloud,' said Garl.

'We will do as you wish,' Visha said. 'Calm yourself. Tell me what has been happening.'

Garl's face moved like a mask that suddenly lived. 'I have found someone. A boy at the school.'

'You told me', said Visha. 'What else?'

'It is hard to explain. I suppose it is almost as though he too has discovered and released something in me. I cannot analyse it.'

'Something in your mind?'

'No, that is the point you see? There are no problems with things of the mind.'

'But if they lie outside the mind', Visha mused, 'we have no words, no ideas, no experience.'

'Correct.'

'Our people have coped with alien experiences before now,' said Visha.

'I know,' said Garl intensely, 'but always by suppressing them. Never before have we allowed them to pass into us. This is new.' His eyes suddenly shone and he smiled broadly. 'This boy must be the mutation. He has to be the one we have been sent to find. Can you think of any other explanation?'

'I can think of nothing for now,' Visha said. 'But give me his name, the names of his parents and whatever else you know. I will need to check records, if I can locate them.'

Garl told her all the details of his contact with Jonathan Wilkes: The time at school, the dreams, the thoughts that had passed between them, and the triumph of that moment when, for the first time, Jonathan's mind had reached out and summoned Garl to the beach.

The following morning Visha took the early morning bus to the nearest town. She was away all day, travelling back that evening on the return journey. She had found out what she needed to know.

At school Jonathan quietly tested himself again and again. Using nothing but his mind he asked Karl to pass him a ruler, then a pencil, then a pen, and each time Karl obliged until Jonathan could no longer concentrate on his work. Mr Lockett had to reprimand him for falling behind and tell him sharply to stop daydreaming.

84

Daydreaming! If only it were just daydreaming! The comfortable fantasy of a daydream which, however far it might range into the impossible, was still under control and could be dissolved in an instant. It was like finding that your secret room had suddenly grown another door, and beyond it lay the unknown which was real. And what if there were things through that door that could bite? Even as he had these thoughts, Jonathan knew for certain now that Karl could read them if he wished, and he felt bare and naked. The suspicions he had seen dawning on Mary's face as she felt herself manipulated made sense to him, and he was glad his instinct had already told him never to do that again.

He remembered the earthquake that had jolted Wilkes Beach a few months before. The cat had known. She had bolted inside with a scrabbling of claws on the kitchen lino and fled desperately to Jonathan's bedroom. There she had crouched at the foot of the dressing table, unable even to seek shelter under the bed. She had lain prone, hissing her fear to anyone who came near, teeth bared and eyes staring yellow. A few minutes later the earthquake had struck with a rapid shudder that was gone almost at once. The cat had known, but she had not known what.

The note read, 'Don't worry.' Karl slid it across the desk to him and looked carefully while he glanced at it. Then Karl lowered an eyelid carefully and raised it. Jonathan gave a hoot of laughter as he realized that Karl was trying to wink.

Mr Lockett said in a loud voice, 'Jonathan, I hope you've settled down by this afternoon. During the lunch hour please try to get out of your system whatever it is that has been making you behave so stupidly this morning.'

And that was what Jonathan did, because the playground had grown solemn and quiet. His old friend, Paul, was withdrawn and worried about something, and Belinda and Susan seemed to want to be by themselves. The playground noises were subdued and hushed, and even Karl kept his distance like a polite stranger. This puzzled Jonathan more than anything because he could not understand why Karl would not wish to talk. 'Don't worry,' the note had said, yet Karl behaved as though it had never been written.

Jonathan was not to know that Karl was waiting. He was waiting for Visha to find out and tell him, and if the answer was 'yes', then it would be a spectacular triumph. Something would have been salvaged from the experiment. It would have been plucked from complete disaster. Beyond that, a question was growing in Karl's mind. He could not understand why he was beginning to feel contented among Jonathan, Paul, Belinda and Susan. It was not supposed to happen. Strange thoughts were creeping into his head, and that was not supposed to happen. He was beginning to feel at home. That had never happened before, not even in the experience of the wisest Ruler of his race. What was he?

Nothing happened until the following weekend, when there was an accident. It was Saturday afternoon. Jonathan was lying on his bed reading, occasionally glancing out of his window at the sea. He noticed Aaron Clark's small boat slowly pushing its way around the headland, just out of reach of the rocks and the breaking waves. Jonathan was bored and could think of nothing he particularly wanted to do.

Then suddenly his mind went blank. A vivid light filled his head. He blinked rapidly but he could see nothing except dazzling light. It grew so intense that he shut his eyes tightly to try to get some relief. At once shapes began to form. He saw the track at the northern end of the beach. It wound around above the rocks, then over the headland and down to a valley. Rising sharply, it passed along the edge of the cliffs that dropped down to Dolphin Bay. Jonathan had often walked around the track. It led to a well known fishing spot, reached by scrambling down a narrow cliff path before arriving at a flat stretch of rock, just out of the grasp of the breakers. The path was narrow and poorly marked in places — safe enough for anyone who knew the way, but dangerous for a stranger.

This path appeared in Jonathan's mind, slowly unfolding as if a movie camera were moving ahead of him. Abruptly the film stopped. He saw before him the edge of the track, broken away with fresh earth and newly bared rock. His gaze was taken to the edge from where he could look down. The cliff dropped steeply to the rocks below. The sea surged in and out, cold and foaming.

A metre below the lip a small tree and some scrubby bushes protruded from the cliff face, sturdy and tough from exposure to the wind and salt spray. Someone was clinging to them, sprawled out and hanging on to every foot and handhold within reach. It was Karl. His face wavered and melted as though the sender could not force it into shape. But it was Karl. The bright dream light faded and Jonathan could see again. He leapt from his bed and ran for the door.

'Where are you off to?' his father asked. 'It'll be lunchtime soon.'

'I've just remembered something. I've got to go out. Back soon!' shouted Jonathan, and he was gone.

He ran as fast as he could, down to the beach, on to the hard sand near the water's edge, and along towards the rocks where the track around the hills began. He was sprinting at first but his brain began to function again once his panic had subsided. He slowed to a steady pace. He had a long run in front of him. He noticed Aaron Clark's boat trailer pulled up on the beach and veered towards it. An old mooring rope lay coiled on the front. Grabbing it without stopping, Jonathan bounded up the first stage of the hill path.

He was panting as he rounded the first headland and his legs ached. The rope kept slipping from his shoulder and bouncing against his legs as he ran. Usually it was a brisk thirty-minute walk to Dolphin Bay, but in less than half that time Jonathan, gasping for breath, was running along the path above the cliffs. He came to the track that led down to the bay. Small stones cascaded everywhere. He almost slipped. He slowed and made his way cautiously down. About halfway to the bottom he saw the broken edge of the track.

Jonathan lay on his stomach and peered over. Karl lay sprawled in the branches of the tree. He looked up and tried to smile. He was helpless and frightened, though he seemed to be in control of himself. He had huddled as close as he could to the cliff. He was lying absolutely still.

'Are you all right? I've got a rope. Don't move!' Jonathan said in one breath.

'I'm not going to move,' Karl replied.

'I'll pull you up with the rope.'

'You can't. I'm too heavy.'

'Yes I can. You're not far down.'

'I'll pull you over the edge.'

'Not if I pass the rope around something,' said Jonathan. 'I'll have a look.'

Karl probably could have clambered up without any help, but the sheer drop below had terrified him and made his arms and legs loose with fright. The roots of the tree that held him reached up and down the slope. In several places, where the wind and rain had eroded the rock, they jutted above the crumbling ground like bony knuckles. Jonathan looped one end of the rope around a tough, gnarled root and knotted it tightly. Then he lowered the other end towards Karl.

'Can you tie it around your waist?'

'I don't know,' said Karl.

'Grab hold of it anyway.'

When the swaying rope touched him, Karl slowly moved his hand and snatched it, gripping it tightly as though trying to squeeze juice from it. Jonathan let down more slack.

'You're all right. Just slide it around your back very slowly and tie it in front. You won't fall.'

Karl inched the rope around his middle, pausing every time the branches quivered. Finally he did it and held the rope tight. Jonathan pulled it taut.

'You're safe now,' he said 'I'll pull you up while you hang on to the roots.'

Slowly Karl crawled up to the track. His knees were scratched and bleeding and he ripped a fingernail on a sharp stone. But he dragged himself over the edge and flopped down on to the ground beside Jonathan. He lay still for a few minutes.

Looking about as Karl calmed himself, Jonathan noticed Aaron's boat below them, easing its way into the rocks with Aaron's head craning back as his mouth moved, trying to shout something that was lost in the noise of the breakers. Jonathan stood up and waved, then pointed to the track back to the beach. He helped Karl to his feet. As they began to walk up the hill he noticed Aaron's boat turning and retracing its course around the headland.

'He must have seen you fall,' said Jonathan.

'He did. I was leaning over watching him. I went too near the edge and it broke away.'

'What were you doing up here?'

'I found an old map in my room, showing some holes in the ground. I was looking for them.'

'Holes in the ground? You mean the foxholes the Home Guard dug in the war?' said Jonathan. 'I could have shown you those. They're almost overgrown now.'

'I can believe that,' said Karl, 'because I didn't find any.'

Karl walked slowly at first but was soon feeling better. He was not injured, apart from a few grazes. 'You reached me quickly,' he said. 'You must have had no trouble in understanding me.'

'I thought my brain was going to blow apart,' said Jonathan.

'I was terrified,' Karl said. 'I could not control myself. I was not sending to you alone. I knew you would see something, but I could not be sure.'

'You were telling your mother?'

Karl hesitated. 'Yes, my mother.'

Like an actress making her entrance on cue, Mrs Smith appeared on the track below them, hurrying upwards. Karl shouted and waved. At once she relaxed, waiting. Karl walked on, then stopped when he realized that Jonathan had not moved.

'What's the matter? You must meet my mother. I know what it is. I have not thanked you. I thank you now for my life. Now come on.'

'It's not that,' Jonathan said.

'What then?'

'You haven't told me everything have you? Who are you? Who is she?' Jonathan pointed to the figure waiting for them down the track.

'Be patient,' said Karl. 'I promise you will know, and you will be glad I waited. Very soon now I will tell you a secret that you will never believe. You must trust me.'

'I suppose I'll have to,' said Jonathan.

He walked down the track beside Karl. When they reached Mrs Smith they stopped. Her deep brown eyes stared at Jonathan intently. She bowed slightly, like a diplomat in a royal court, but she said nothing. Her son, thought Jonathan, has been rescued from almost certain death — and she says nothing.

'You go on,' said Karl. 'I'll be all right now, but I think I should walk slowly.'

When Jonathan was out of earshot, Karl said excitedly, 'That is the one. That is Jonathan Wilkes, the boy I was telling you about. He is the one!'

Visha turned to Garl. 'No, it is not him. It cannot be him.'

'But it must be!'

'No. I have checked the records. Remember we know the approximate time that it happened. I have read the records of births and deaths. This boy could not be the one.'

'Did you go back through enough years?'

'I made no mistake,' said Visha. 'Their records are kept in a court house. I was able to read their names of births and deaths going back many years, even beyond the time we are interested in. The grandparents would be the ones who fit. They were not here at the right time. I even checked on the great-grand-parents.'

Visha looked at Garl with something almost approaching concern on her face. 'I am right,' she said. 'I could have told you two days ago but I wanted to be sure. I even examined the dates on the headstones in the cemetery and other records in the church. The family does not fit.'

Garl pointed to Jonathan's disappearing back. 'Then how do you explain him?'

'I do not know,' Visha muttered, 'but whatever the explanation, he is none of our doing.'

'Then who is responsible?'

'Wouldn't it be strange,' Visha replied, 'if it happened of its own accord? All this trouble, and it would have happened anyway.'

'It would be very strange,' said Garl, nodding. 'But

think about this. If Jonathan Wilkes is not the one, who is? Believe me, there is someone. I can feel it. There is someone here, I am certain.'

They continued down the track. When they came to the top of the slope that brought them into plain view of the beach, they saw Jonathan talking to Aaron Clark beside his boat, pulled up on the sand. Frank Gibbons was replacing a coil of rope on the boat trailer. At the appearance of the two the figures below were suddenly frozen, staring upwards like people caught motionless in a painting. Visha said, 'Now I must decide how I should behave as a mother of a son who has been rescued from almost certain death.'

Garl wrote the second section of the report in a linked script, forming the loops and tails of the letters with care and concentration. As he wrote, he found his hand moving more easily. He made his muscles relax.

2.   *Instructions to the First Close Contact Expedition*
2.1 *The four members of the first expedition were instructed to establish themselves in a human community and study the inhabitants. They were to carry out two major tasks:*
*(a)  To discover and record as much information as possible about the social life of the species in order to add to the store of knowledge we had already gained. For example, we already knew the nature of the major languages spoken on the planet, but we lacked close knowledge of the unspoken, or body language that possibly existed among them. We needed to know more about the ways human beings behaved towards each other.*
*(b)  To study the minds of several chosen specimens of the race and to discover, if possible, what their mental*

*capabilities were. We were especially interested to know how the biological evolution of the human brain differed from that of closely related species. In brief, what was the human mind capable of doing?*

*2.2 The members of the expedition were strictly forbidden to interfere with the specimens chosen for study in any way that would damage them, or even make them aware that they had been singled out for attention. They were to use instruments in remote phase only, together with their own powers of mental analysis.*

*2.3 Upon their departure, no evidence was to remain of their visit, apart from hidden signalling devices which might be required by future close contact expeditions to the same locality.*

*2.4 The location chosen was to be in a remote spot, likely to remain isolated for as long as possible.*

Garl put down the pencil and flexed his fingers. He returned the papers to his desk drawer with a satisfied smile.

# VIII

## SCATTERED STONES

Frank had to go away for two days on a buying trip. He did not want to go, but several weeks earlier he had heard about an old church in a town some distance away with a great deal of lead in its roof. The building was to be demolished. An old friend on the parish committee had thought of Frank when the subject of the sale of the metal had come up for discussion. Mr Gibbons of Wilkes Beach had been successful in his tender. But the demolition team hired to haul the building apart found it could begin work two weeks earlier than expected, and Frank suddenly found that if he wanted a truck load of lead, he would have to be on the spot at once.

He was reluctant to leave. He had a premonition of danger, a sense that he should not leave Myra. But he had done so before, frequently, and could think of no logical reason why he should not go now. He had been hoarding his petrol coupons and had enough fuel for the truck. Yet an image kept coming back to him. The two Smiths walking over the brow of the hill and pausing at the top of the track that sloped down to the beach, their ivory pale faces and blond hair — and dark, staring eyes. Their eyes from a distance looked like empty black sockets.

Frank knew that his reaction was primitive. Young Jonathan Wilkes had told him what had happened and he had spoken as a friend of the boy he had rescued.

On Aaron's face there had been nothing but concern. He had seen Karl's fall, but from his rocking boat had been able to do nothing except scream advice. Jonathan's appearance at the cliff top had seemed to him a miracle. But Frank felt an emotion stirring that frightened him. The faces of the two strange people roused memories of hollow-eyed skulls. He felt fear and hatred, and of these the most frightening was the urge to hate. He was a gentle man. He had seen and heard many hateful things in his life. But never before had he sensed this emotion within himself, so strong that he felt his muscles flex and stiffen involuntarily when he thought of it.

He understood the cause. Myra's life had been jarred and shaken by these two people in a way he could not comprehend. Because he did not know, he feared them; because it was Myra who seemed threatened, he discovered he could also hate. That was why he almost decided to forget about the truck load of lead. But then he saw that he had not a single solid reason to stay. He would be away for two days. The profit would be good. Above all, Myra was happy that he should make the trip. She was in no doubt. As always, there were neighbours and friends all round her in case of emergency. He had gone away on similar trips countless times before. What was so different this time?

Perhaps it was the thought of having to give a convincing answer to that question that finally decided Frank. He climbed into his truck early in the morning and drove away, promising to be back the following night. In the late afternoon of the day of his departure, Myra was found to be missing.

The discovery was made by Paul. He had taken

to heart Frank's request to keep an eye on Myra and, ever since, he had watched her comings and goings up Church Street with great care. He even took to wandering around behind her at a distance whenever she went to the shops, and had come to convince himself that her safety depended on him. His mother had strict instructions to note Myra's activities when he was at school, and his first task on returning home was to learn if Myra had made her daily visit to the headstones. In fact, his mother was becoming exasperated by his keenness and more than once suggested that he go and play with Jonathan or one of his other friends.

The day Frank went away was a school day. That afternoon Paul dashed home as usual. 'Has she been up the road yet?' he asked his mother.

'If she has, I haven't seen her.'

'Mr Gibbons went away this morning. I think I'll go down the road and have a look around.'

'Paul,' said his mother, 'there's no need to fuss. I want you to do an errand for me.'

But he had gone. He walked down to the end of the street, across the main road, past Jonathan's house, then towards the street leading to the beach where Frank and Myra lived. He walked casually, seeming to be going nowhere in particular, and waved to Mrs Wilkes, who was standing at her kitchen window.

As soon as he reached the gate of the Gibbons property he knew the cottage was empty. He could see both the front and back doors at the same time from a certain point on the road. They were shut. There was no sign of the cat sunning herself on the back porch. The clothes line was bare. Paul had never realized before how, over the years, these little signs of warmth and occupancy had become so familiar to him. Their absence struck him at once.

He would have to check. He remembered his mother's request, heard faintly as he had scampered through the front gate, and decided that he would knock on Myra's back door. If she did answer he could ask if she wanted any errands done. The cottage was silent. He stood at the back door. There was no sound from inside. He knocked softly, then louder, and listened for approaching footsteps. Nothing. The silence was so bare and empty that he could just detect the sound of the kitchen clock ticking.

Paul waited. He was about to give up and go away, but ventured one last try. He had never before opened the door of anyone's house uninvited, but now he swallowed, gripped the handle and pushed the door ajar. He called very quickly, 'Mrs Gibbons! Are you there? Mum said I should ask if you want any errands done.'

His words fell flat in the silence. There was no one in the house. Shutting the door, he walked quickly out the gate and ran home.

'She's not there!' he shouted, as he burst through the door.

'Who's not where?' his mother inquired.

'Mrs Gibbons! She's gone. There's no one at home!'

'Perhaps she's down at the shops.'

'Oh, I didn't think of that,' said Paul.

'Speaking of shops, I want you to get me some butter. Here's the money. Off you go.'

In a slightly easier frame of mind, Paul walked down to the store. It was silly of him not to have thought of it himself. Myra was hardly a house-bound invalid.

All the same, he would have a good look around. He bought his mother's butter and strolled along the footpath. There was no sign of Myra. He returned home by walking a short way along the beach, then across the sand dunes and up the street where Myra lived. He did not see her. There was no change in the appearance of the house. Paul was quiet as he continued home.

Then he had another thought. The cemetery. He should have thought of going there first. He ran up the road and walked quickly around the side of the church along a well worn track. There was no one seated among the headstones, no grey-haired figure sitting at the foot of a grave, rocking gently backwards and forwards, smiling quietly to herself. Myra was not there.

Later that evening, after dark, Paul crept from the house and once more went down the road. He had no need to go right up to the door this time. The Gibbons cottage was in complete darkness. There were no lights at any window.

This time his mother looked apprehensive when he told her. His father took a torch and left the house. He opened the door of Myra's cottage, as Paul had done, and called. When he heard no reply and then saw in the beam of his torch an unwashed plate in the kitchen sink, encrusted with the remains of breakfast cereal, he raised the alarm.

Jonathan heard the knock on the door from his bedroom, then the sound of muffled voices. Curious, he walked out into the main room to find it empty. He craned his neck around the kitchen door to see his parents on the back porch talking quietly to Paul's father. He heard the words 'police', 'first thing tomorrow morning,' and 'search,' and waited impatiently for someone to return inside and tell him what was happening.

Mrs Wilkes came into the kitchen alone, looking worried.

'What's the matter?' Jonathan hissed.

His mother looked up, startled. 'What? Oh, it's you. Mrs Gibbons seems to be missing from home.'

'Myra?'

'Yes, Myra. There's no one answering the door.'

'She might be up at the cemetery. Paul said the other day that she's started going up there after dark.'

'Paul looked there earlier on,' said Mrs Wilkes.

'Paul?'

'Yes. He was the one who discovered that she isn't at home.'

'Where can she be then?' said Jonathan. 'What do you think has happened to her?'

'We don't know that anything has happened to her,' Mrs Wilkes replied, 'and we can't do much before morning anyway. Your father is going across to the cottage to have a good look, just in case she's fallen somewhere and knocked herself out.'

Mr Wilkes came back about half an hour later. When he saw their inquiring faces he shook his head. 'No sign of her. We searched the house, then we walked around the shops.'

'Someone must have seen her,' said Mrs Wilkes.

'Possibly they did, but we won't be able to find out until morning.'

'Will you phone the police?'

'I already have, from the store. Ted Burns said he

would come out from town himself first thing tomorrow morning.'

'What about Frank? Shouldn't we let him know what's happened?'

'If I knew where to get in touch with him, I would,' said Mr Wilkes, 'but he doesn't seem to have told anyone where he was going this trip, apart from Myra. He's due back late tomorrow anyway and I doubt if anyone could track him down before then.'

Sergeant Ted Burns was officer-in-charge of the nearest police station, in the town over the hills. Wilkes Beach was rarely in need of law enforcement, certainly not among the permanent residents. The summer months saw an occasional police constable making the rounds, mainly to watch for any holidaymakers who might decide to prolong New Year's Eve celebrations. At other times Jonathan's father seemed to be the unspoken representative of law and order in the community. If help were needed, people always approached him to do something about it. He said it was the fault of their name. It made them seem the owners of the town and in times of need people always turned to the lord of the manor for help.

On his way to school next morning Jonathan saw the police car roll down the main road and stop outside the Post Office, next to Wilkes' General Store. Like every other child in the school he bemoaned the fact that today of all days had to be a school day, just when something like this had happened. If there was going to be a search he wanted to see what was going on.

All day they waited for three o'clock when school would be dismissed. Paul waited anxiously because he

101

was vaguely afraid that if Myra were not found he would feel responsible. He knew he was not to blame, but knowing did not help much. Jonathan wondered if Karl might know anything, but he could tell that Karl had no knowledge whatever of what might have happened. When they chatted about Myra's disappearance Jonathan could sense that Karl was hiding nothing and was, in fact, puzzled.

But he noticed that Susan and Belinda were secretive, talking quietly together and falling silent when anyone came near them in the playground. He wished he knew what they were discussing.

They were talking about a marvellous idea suggested by a chance remark from Susan. She had said to Belinda as they arrived at school, 'I wonder if they brought tracker dogs.'

'Who?'

'The police.'

'I wonder,' said Belinda.

By morning break Belinda's imagination had done its work and she could hardly wait to drag Susan away from the others.

'If the police haven't brought any dogs, suppose you and I help out with a dog of our own,' she whispered excitedly.

'We don't own a dog,' Susan pointed out.

'I know we don't,' snapped Belinda, 'but there's nothing to stop us borrowing one.'

'Who would lend us a dog?'

'We'll ask Mr Madsen for Blue.'

'Blue? Old Blue?' Susan giggled. 'What use would he be?'

'Well, I just thought it would be a good idea,' said

Belinda. 'After all, he is supposed to be a sheep dog, and even if he is old he might have enough sniff left in him to pick up a scent. But if you're not interested ...'

'No, wait a minute,' said Susan. 'It could be a good idea. I didn't mean to laugh. It sounded so strange. The only thing is ...'

'What?'

'Are you sure you aren't making it sound like a game or something? I mean, what if something *has* happened to Myra, and we use it for an excuse to play around and pretend we're doing something important?'

Belinda thought for a moment. 'You're right,' she said, 'but we don't have to think of it as a game. It's more of a disguise really.'

'What do you mean?'

'Would your parents or mine really let us join in a search?'

'I doubt it,' said Susan.

'So do I. But if they saw us with Blue and we said we were taking him for a walk, they'd have no idea what we were really doing, would they?'

Susan smiled. 'You mean we'd be children disguising ourselves as children.'

'Exactly!'

When school was over everyone scattered for home to get the latest news. One look at his mother's face as he crashed through the door told Jonathan all he needed to know. She looked worried. Myra had not been found.

'I'm glad you're home early,' his mother said. 'Dad's out helping search around the cliff track and had to close the store this afternoon. I'm going down to open up for a couple of hours and I want you to look after Mary.'

Jonathan was on the point of protesting but realized it might not be wise. 'Will it be all right if I take her down to the beach?' If he could manage that, at least he might be able to see what was going on.

'Yes, if you want to, but make sure you're home by five o'clock.'

Belinda and Susan ran to their homes, quickly dumped their schoolbags and met, breathless, at their rendezvous outside the Madsen farm. Mrs Madsen answered their knock.

'Hello girls. Is there any news?'

'I don't think so. They're still looking,' Susan said.

'I do hope she's all right. They've been searching since morning, you know. I haven't seen Conrad all day.'

'We wondered if we could take Blue for a walk,' said Belinda.

'Blue? Well, I suppose you can. He could do with some exercise. But why do you want to do that?'

'Just something to do,' said Susan.

'We'd fidget if we sat around at home,' Belinda said.

'I know how you feel. All right then, but you had better take the leash. That old dog is probably too lazy to run away, but he likes chasing seagulls on the beach if he's in the mood, and you might have trouble keeping up with him.'

They set off with Blue trailing behind them back down the road to the village centre.

'Where shall we go first?'

'Along the beach,' said Belinda. 'I want to see what's happening down by the cliffs.'

'Seeing we have Blue with us anyway, I think we ought to give him a try. You never know, he might scent something.'

'You mean we could walk past the Gibbons' house on the way to the beach?'

'That's what I had in mind,' Susan replied. 'We have to walk down one of the roads to get to the beach and it might as well be that one.'

'I can't see anything childish in that idea,' Belinda said. 'We'll do it.'

Blue walked in the rear, tongue lolling out as though it had become unfastened, his tail gently wagging as he enjoyed his afternoon stroll.

'Of course,' said Susan, looking behind her, 'if Blue were tracking someone he should be in front.'

'Like a bloodhound.'

Susan nodded. 'You always see bloodhounds in front.'

They tried, but Blue did not want to walk in front. After a lifetime of being told to 'get in behind' and 'heel boy, heel!' he was not about to take chances with new-fangled ideas. He had learnt from bitter experience that his master did not appreciate it when he used his initiative, like taking a short cut when bringing in sheep. Blue walked a determined three paces to the rear and nothing could persuade him to move up front.

Belinda looked at him thoughtfully. 'I think Blue is going to have ornamental value only. Never mind.'

But Blue's big moment was soon to come. They had almost reached Jonathan's house when Susan noticed Karl standing at the entrance of Church Street looking down at the beach.

She waved and called. 'Hello Karl! We're going for a walk. Want to come?'

He joined them, smiling shyly. 'I'd like to. Everyone seems so unsettled today. I was curious to see what was happening.'

'Myra hasn't been found,' Belinda said. 'Everyone is worried. That's why they're unsettled.'

'I know that, of course. It just seems so strange that no one can do anything.'

'There's not much you can do except search.'

'And hope,' Susan added.

'I don't think I know this woman, Myra,' Karl said. 'What does she look like?'

'Mrs Gibbons?' said Susan. 'You must have seen her. She often goes up to the cemetery by the church, opposite your house. She's a sweet old lady with grey hair.'

Karl nodded thoughtfully. 'Ah yes, I think I know who you mean and I believe I have seen her. Yes, I know I have seen her. So she is the one who is missing.'

'You can see her house from here,' Belinda said. 'Come on, we're going down to the beach and we'll have a quick glance as we go past.'

They turned the corner of the street, past the Wilkes' house, and walked down the rough, grassed verge towards the gate of the Gibbons' cottage. Then it happened. The cottage was quiet with no sign of life, except one. Myra's cat was drowsing on the mat before the front door, probably wondering why she had not been invited inside. She chose the exact moment when the small group was passing the gate to stand up and stretch in full view.

Perhaps Blue was tired of the monotony of trudging along on the end of a leash, or perhaps he decided that he disliked this particular cat, though he paid little attention to the ones on the farm. Whatever the reason, he uttered a deep-throated bark, snatched the lead from Susan's hand and charged.

Cat and dog circled the house twice before Belinda and Susan managed to corner Blue on the back lawn. The cat had disappeared. Blue wagged his tail happily and began to trot towards the girls, his rebellion completely evaporated. Then suddenly he turned aside and nosed at the foot of a large tree growing on the lawn. It was a magnificent shade tree and Frank had built a small seat against its trunk. Blue's nose was sniffing at the grass beside the seat. Then he decided he had not discovered anything of importance and continued on his way.

'You heartless animal,' said Belinda, taking the leash firmly in her hand.

Karl, who had hung back while the noise of the chase rang in the air, came forward timidly. 'He seems very savage.'

'Not really. He was having fun. He could never have caught up with the cat, and they both knew it.'

'Belinda!'

Susan had walked over to see what Blue had been investigating. Her shout startled them. Belinda and Karl ran to the base of the tree. On the ground before the wooden seat lay Myra's jewel box. Beside it, scattered over a small patch of grass, were the coloured stones. Their colours glowed warmly in the late afternoon sun, and on several of them tiny flecks of some mineral glinted like sparks of fire.

Belinda and Susan looked at each other, mouths hanging open.

'Myra's stones,' whispered Belinda.

'Her greatest treasure.'

'What are they doing out here?'

'She must have brought them out,' said Susan slowly. 'She must have been sitting on the bench . . . '

'Looking at them,' Belinda continued, 'and then she dropped them.'

'Or threw them down.'

'Yes, you're right. They're scattered. She threw them down. She threw them down on the grass and dropped the box.'

'But she would never do that!'

'She did! She did! And now she's gone.'

Karl stared at the stones as though they hypnotized him. He was aware of the girls talking but he did not hear them. The coloured orbs glowed like primitive replicas of the flaming spheres that hung in cold, dark space, and at once his intuition told him who Myra was and where she had gone.

He heard Belinda say, 'She must have been upset. She must have rushed off somewhere.'

'What should we do?' Susan asked.

'We'll have to tell someone.'

'I have to go,' Karl said sharply. 'I am expected at home. I don't think I can help you.'

'That's all right,' said Belinda. She had almost forgotten that Karl was there. 'Sorry if we sound excited, but it's something you wouldn't understand anyway.'

108

'See you tomorrow,' called Susan after him as he walked away.

Once out of sight, Karl walked quickly up the road then broke into a run as he neared his own gate. Inside, he went quickly to the bathroom and removed his eye shields, which always began hurting at this time of day. Then he found Visha.

'Did you leave the house at any time today?'

'This morning,' said Visha. 'I was out for about two hours. I wanted to see what this search was concerned with. There is a woman missing, isn't there?'

Garl nodded. 'There is a woman missing. You know her. You have seen her. She came to our door.'

'You mean the strange woman,' said Visha, 'the one who seemed lost?'

'She is the one,' Garl replied.

'Tell me what you know. You know something don't you?'

Garl looked at her. 'This time I know. This time I can feel it.'

Visha nodded. 'There has been something different here since morning. I took no notice. It is not the first time it has happened, but before now it was always something normal we had simply not expected — a cat, a mouse, an owl.'

She looked at Garl and waited, inviting him to lead. He did not hesitate. He took her out the back door to the squat, brick outbuilding — the original cottage. A connecting door led into the room that was now a laundry, but he did not go near that. He walked around the concrete path that skirted the building to a door at the rear. It opened into a large room that had once been two small bedrooms. With the dividing wall removed it now provided a large space that was used as a junk room, with one corner reserved for storing gardening equipment. Over the years, unused furniture and household goods had accumulated there, settling themselves into a dusty, contorted, slumbering nest. The sinking sun glowed yellow through the cobwebbed windows.

They could see at once that things had been moved and pushed aside. A roll of carpet reared up, where it had lain flat before. Two broken kitchen chairs sat out on the concrete floor, a table had been pushed aside, and streaks and patches of varnish on wooden surfaces glowed in the golden light where the deep dust had been recently disturbed.

From where he stood, Garl could see a reason for the moving and shifting. A kind of avenue had been created, leading towards the far corner of the room. He eased his way towards it, clambering over the furniture and boxes until he could see into the furthest gloom.

In the corner stood an old bed with a bare mattress spread out, still curled at the ends from being rolled tightly for decades. Myra was sitting on the mattress, leaning back against the wall. She rocked gently from side to side. Her eyes were half closed. On her face was a look of utter contentment and peace, like the expression of a small child in its own room who has returned home at last from a journey that has lasted far too long.

'She is the one,' Garl breathed softly. He turned to Visha. 'She is the one we have been searching for.'

# IX

# PRISONERS

Garl picked up the pen and dipped the nib slowly into the bottle of ink. He had experimented and learned to apply just the right pressure on the paper so that the ink made a smooth, unbroken line with no blobs. He had discovered that the angle the nib made against the page governed the thickness of the line. As he wrote, he recalled the sentence he had read somewhere, 'The words flowed from his pen'. Until now, he had not really understood what those words meant.

3.   *The Outcome of the First Contact Expedition*

3.1  *The expedition was a disaster. The leader of the party exceeded his powers and deliberately disobeyed one of the fundamental principles followed by our civilization — never to interfere in the natural growth and evolution of an alien race. The members of this expedition tampered with members of the human race.*

3.2  *Unfortunately, the full records of what exactly happened during the expedition's stay on the third planet have been lost. Their destruction occurred soon after the return of the expedition. How that happened need not concern you, though the death of the group's leader is common knowledge and you would be correct in assuming that the loss of the official records was closely connected with the decease of this individual.*

3.3  *However, information given by surviving members of the party does provide us with a certain number of facts.*

*(a) We know the precise location of the community where the members of the expedition established themselves. There is a guide beacon in place which is still active. This will enable you to find the same landing circle used by the first expedition.*

*(b) The dwelling place used originally will possibly be easy to find, provided that the nàtural environment has not changed too greatly. We know that it was almost surrounded by the natural vegetation of the planet, and that a burial ground was located nearby.*

*(c) We are certain beyond any doubt that the tampering with a number of native inhabitants took the form of a genetic transplant performed in the region of the brain that controls language. The survivors claimed that the intention was to discover if the minds of human beings could be made to understand and use the techniques of thought transfer which we use frequently to communicate. It was claimed by the survivors of the expedition that the human brain seemed, physically, an almost exact replica of our own. They were therefore tempted to provide the genetic codes which, they hoped, would jolt the minds of human beings into a further stage of development, matching the capabilities of our own. In other words, they deliberately interfered with the process of natural evolution. They acted like gods.*

*(d) The operations (we know there was more than one) were performed using the standard laboratory equipment carried by our intermediate range scout ships, though this would have been sufficient if the operator were an expert in this field. This was not the case on this occasion.*

*(e) We do not know the identities of the human beings on whom these transplant operations were performed.*

*(f) The genetic material used in the transplants came from the brain tissue of the leader of the First Contact Expedition. (g) On the time scale of the third planet, the operations were probably performed in the year 1893 or 1894.*

Garl looked at the disciplined beauty of the written page with the pride of a craftsman. Then he began the final section.

Although darkness had fallen, it was one of those evenings when parents put aside bedtime routines and do not seem to mind if a few dishes wait in the sink until next morning. The children flitted through the darkness to each other's houses and peered from darkened windows without a mother's or father's voice going off like an alarm clock.

Unable to stay at home thinking while his parents chatted over a fence to neighbours, Paul sought out Jonathan. Together they knelt on Jonathan's bed and looked down the road to the Gibbons' cottage. They saw Mrs Wilkes moving in and out the brightly lit back door as she bustled about making sure that everything in Myra's home was settled for the night.

A police car rolled quietly down the street and stopped outside the gate. They could see the light glinting on the police officer's uniform insignia as he went inside, then emerged a few minutes later. The car moved away and turned right toward the Post Office. By now there were three police vehicles at Wilkes Beach. Craning their necks, Paul and Jonathan could just make out their dark shapes parked under the street lights and the vague shadows of people moving back and forth.

'They brought in a lot more police this afternoon,' Paul whispered.

'I know,' Jonathan replied. 'I heard Dad say that everyone who can help is going to be searching tomorrow. They might even close the school.'

'Why?'

'I think it's because they want the building to organize things. We haven't got a hall and the Post Office isn't big enough.'

Paul blinked rapidly. 'I wonder what's happened to her.'

'She'll be all right,' said Jonathan firmly. 'She must be. They've been around all the dangerous places. They've searched the cliffs and the tracks over the hill. Dad said so. He was with them.'

'Look! There's Mr Lockett.'

They glanced to the left and saw Mr Lockett walk through the pocket of light spread by the street lamp outside, then merge into shadow and darkness as he hurried down the road.

'He must be going to the Post Office.'

'They'll be talking about using the school tomorrow,' Paul said. 'I don't want school to be cancelled. I never thought I'd say that.'

'Myra will be all right.'

'What will Frank say?' Paul whispered. 'What do you think he'll say? I promised I'd watch out for her. What do you think he'll say to me?'

'He won't say anything,' said Jonathan. 'If he blames anyone, he'll blame himself for not being here. Mum thinks so anyway. That's why they're all waiting out there now pretending to be busy.'

'Who? I can't see anyone except your mother . . . '

'And the people at the Post Office and the police cars cruising up and down the road, and I'll bet Belinda and Susan aren't very far away.'

'They had Blue earlier on. They said they were taking him for a walk.'

'I know,' Jonathan said. 'Fat chance they would have had finding anything with him!'

'I'm going outside to have a look. And I'd better show up at home for a while in case I'm wanted. Are you coming?'

'Mary's in bed,' Jonathan said. 'I've got to look after her. Anyway, I can see what's happening from here.'

'See you later.'

Almost as soon as Paul had gone Jonathan felt it once more — a slight brightening of light behind his eyes, a pale version of the glare that had rocked his head on the day Karl had fallen over the cliff. This time it had been like an intruder who had peeped through a door and retreated on seeing that the room was occupied. Then it came again. He felt Karl calling him, drawing him quietly and urgently, and an image of the Smiths' house swam in his eyes.

Jonathan was about to run from the room when he thought of Mary. He could not leave her. He sank back on the bed and brought Mary's sleeping shape to his mind, holding it firmly. The light behind his eyes faded slowly. He understood. Karl would be calling again.

At that moment the waiting darkness was disturbed by a distant growl as Frank's truck burst free of the last hairpin bend and surged on to the long stretch of straight road that ran the length of Wilkes Beach.

Frank pushed the accelerator to the floor but the

truck, weighed down by a heavy load, still stayed below the speed limit. Frank was weary. Ever since leaving Wilkes Beach the previous morning he had worked until his muscles strained, and now they ached as he slumped in his seat and steered for home. He was almost ready to breathe a sigh of relief, giving thanks for an uneventful two days with his worst fears unfounded, when he saw in his headlights a car pass him going in the opposite direction. He had time to see the word 'Police' in white letters on the driver's door. He saw its headlights in his rear vision mirror swing to the right as it made a U-turn and speeded up to catch and follow him. The police car accompanied him to his front gate like a shepherd. When he drove in and stepped from the truck, Frank saw two policemen walking up the path. One look at Sergeant Ted Burns' face was enough.

'It's Myra, isn't it Ted? Something has happened to Myra.' He spoke the words slowly and evenly as though jabbing each one separately and deliberately into his brain. 'Something has happened to Myra.'

Sergeant Burns nodded. 'You'd better come inside Frank. Myra's been missing since yesterday. We've spent all day searching.'

The next hour passed by Frank in a parade of faces and words, a flow of people who moved around him as he sat in his chair, like performers in a parade, all talking to him and telling him what had happened. He caught a phrase here and there and tried to respond. He discovered a mug of tea in his hand and thought how strange it was that he should be drinking tea without sugar, but he didn't complain. He nodded and listened and heard himself answering questions, but he found himself staring at the wall. Finally his eyes were fixed on the mantlepiece because all the words had finished jabbing and pecking and his brain was numb and he could hear nothing.

But he nodded when Frank Burns said, 'We'll be round to collect you first thing in the morning, Frank.'

And he smiled when Jonathan's mother patted him on the shoulder and said, 'Get off to bed Frank. You look worn out. Don't worry, I'm sure she's safe inside somewhere. We'll find her.'

He stared at the mantlepiece as the house emptied and the worried faces disappeared into the dark. In the silence Frank stirred and slowly watched the room settle back around him, like a favourite cardigan snuggling over his shoulders. But his eyes would not leave the mantlepiece. They passed along the cluttered array of ornaments, vases and shells, then back again. Now Frank was concentrating. He looked again.

His cry of triumph as he leapt to his feet was almost drowned by a squeal of fright from the doorway. He turned to see Belinda and Susan wide-eyed with fear, ready to run — and there it was in Susan's hand. The wooden jewel box.

Frank smiled. 'I'm sorry, I'm sorry,' he said. 'I didn't mean to frighten you. I had no idea you were there. You're not really scared are you?'

Belinda recovered quickly. 'Not in the least,' she said, gulping quickly. 'Not now anyway.'

'You see,' Frank chuckled, 'you made your entrance just when I noticed that wasn't on the mantlepiece.' He pointed to the box then moved over and lifted the lid. 'They're all there are they? I wouldn't know how many stones there are supposed to be.'

'We think we found them all,' said Susan.

'Found them? Where did you find them? No, wait a minute, let's sit down quietly while you tell me all about it.' Then another thought struck him. 'But shouldn't you two be at home? Do Mum and Dad know you're here?'

'We sneaked out,' Belinda said, grinning. 'It'll be all right, though. They're still wandering around talking and we'll be home again before they know we're not there.'

So they told him about Blue chasing the cat around the house and how he had led them to the stones scattered on the lawn. They had gathered them and restored them to their box and kept them safe until they could return them to the mantlepiece.

'And so here they are,' said Frank softly. 'Now isn't that an amazing thing. Tell me what you think happened.'

'Myra — Mrs Gibbons — must have . . .'

'Let's call her Myra,' said Frank. 'Let's forget about Mr and Mrs. I think Myra sounds much better.'

Susan began again. 'Myra must have taken the box outside and sat on the bench looking at the stones.'

'She's never done that before,' Frank muttered. 'She's always spread them on this table, never anywhere else.'

'Perhaps she wanted to see the sunlight on them,' Belinda suggested.

'Perhaps she did,' Frank nodded. 'Never mind, what do you think happened next?'

'She threw them on the ground.'

'She threw them. Why couldn't she have dropped

118

them? Why couldn't they have slipped from her hands and on to the grass at her feet?'

Belinda leaned forward. 'Because they were scattered, weren't they Susan?'

'Yes, they were, as though she'd flung them into the air. Belinda's right, Mr Gibbons.'

Frank pursed his lips. 'So that brings up the really interesting question. Why would she have thrown them away from her?'

The girls were silent. They were being led into territory where adults behaved mysteriously, talking darkly in voices mumbling from behind closed doors.

'We don't know,' said Belinda at last.

'Those stones are treasures,' Susan said. 'Why would anyone throw away treasures? We couldn't understand either.'

Frank looked at their worried faces and realized that the anxiety he was feeling belonged to him alone. He had no business letting them feel the distress that was filling him.

'Well,' he said with a grin. 'I'm sure we'll work it out. And I'll tell you something else. I think you've been a big help, I really do.' He took their hands. 'Now, I think you two should get off home. Shall we see if we can find a biscuit to help you on your way?'

He ushered them from the house and waved from the back door as they walked to the gate. When they were out of earshot Susan said, 'Do you want my biscuit?'

Belinda shook her head. 'No, I was going to give you mine.'

'He was trying to laugh it off, wasn't he?'

'Yes,' said Belinda, 'but sometimes you've got to let them think you believe them. It just seems kinder that way occasionally.'

Frank closed the door, went back to his armchair and resumed staring at the mantlepiece, with the wooden casket now back in place. But now he was alert. His mind was working. What reason could Myra possibly have for casting aside her precious stones? Because she no longer wanted them. Or rather, at some precise moment she no longer felt the need of them. Why? Because she had suddenly become aware of something far more valuable. But what? Perhaps she did not know exactly, but merely knew where she might look for it. If the girls were right, her actions spoke of someone who had suddenly decided to go somewhere, spurred by an impulse that pushed everything else aside.

Where might that be? As he pondered the question the answer grew like a swelling wave. He knew without a doubt where the solution lay. What the answer would be remained hidden.

Frank went outside to his workshop and rummaged in the dark depths of an old tin chest that lay half-hidden in a far corner. He reached down and removed a long case. He took it back inside to the dining table, eased open the rusty clips and lifted the lid. The twin barrels of a shot-gun gleamed in the light. Alongside, the wooden stock snuggled in its clamps. He removed the two parts of the weapon and fitted them together, then broke the barrels and peered through them at the light bulb. They had gathered a film of dust on their oiled surfaces, collected over the many years the gun had been unused. Frank rested the weapon in his hand, gazing at the engraving on the metal he had not seen for so many years, and admiring the intricate carving on the stock. He had forgotten what it looked like.

Then he remembered why. Myra had insisted that she could never live in the same house as any gun, or a weapon of any kind. It was the first time Frank has seen the calm determination in her eyes. He discovered later that she displayed it only rarely, much to his relief, because he quickly came to know that look. It meant that argument was impossible and that in the matter under discussion Myra's wish was a rock wall which could not be battered down. So Frank had hidden the gun and, as he looked at it now for the first time in many years, he knew that to restore it to life was more than his peace of mind was worth.

Frank returned the gun to its case and replaced it in the chest. Going inside, he switched off all the lights. As he shut the back door he began turning the key to lock it, then thought better of it. He put the key in his pocket then quickly walked out the gate and up the street.

Frank was found to be missing the following morning. Mrs Wilkes went across to the cottage soon after breakfast to see how he was 'coping with the day,' as she put it. When no one answered her knock she stepped inside, calling out to him. She moved hesitantly into the silent kitchen and noticed that the sink and bench were completely dry. No one had turned on a tap for several hours. She walked boldly into the living room, calling once more, then peeped through the open bedroom door.

She said afterwards, 'I thought he might have collapsed from shock or something, but the bed hadn't been slept in.'

'And you looked right through the house?' Mr Wilkes asked.

'There was no one there,' she said.

That was all Jonathan heard. His father left for the school where the searchers were to assemble, and his mother departed soon afterwards to open the shop. Mary accompanied her, much to Jonathan's relief. He fully expected to be asked to look after her for the day, but Mary had pleaded to go with her mother, promising to be good. When the door closed behind them the house was silent, and Jonathan waited.

He was waiting to be summoned. He lay on his bed staring at the ceiling, a little frightened. Buzzing insects outside his window roused themselves like tiny saws cutting the air. The day was warming as the sun climbed, but he felt cold. The wallpaper felt chilled and the edges of the window-sill were sharp and hard.

Without warning the room seemed to melt and grow dim around him. Dark pictures suddenly filled his mind. Then he was immersed in an immense freezing blackness with single orbs of brilliant colours slowly swirling and revolving, as far as his mind could see, stretching into pinpricks of light on the borders of infinity. He was watching a silent dance of lights.

Jonathan knew he was being shown the universe in motion as no human eye could ever see it because no human had ever been there, and no human could live long enough to know the rhythms of time it danced to.

Even its stillness seemed solid, as though he could touch it, and of all those brilliant spheres, not one sprayed any rays of light. The icy blackness sucked at the very edges of every one. The stars did not twinkle. They whirled in their galaxies like stones.

And then Jonathan saw drifting towards him a dark globe, a dead moon, that slowly shrouded his vision until everything before him was blotted out except for specks of light on its jagged surface. They swelled in size until they resembled the faint light of torches beamed through a black crystal lens. He felt one swoop upon him. He was carried beneath the surface and at once he was in a world of warmth and light and life.

Encased in the dead crust of the asteroid there was life. There were people with pale blue eyes and white skins and blond hair that shimmered in the perpetual evening light. A softness filled the labyrinth of chambers, rooms and mighty halls. He felt a sense of peace and contentment, mingled with yearning, that he knew did not belong to him.

He heard Karl's voice whisper, 'I was homesick, but I wanted you to see anyway.'

Then Jonathan saw a small group of men and women, some young, some old, who looked and dressed the same as everyone else he had seen except for the chain they wore around their necks. Suspended from each strand was a cluster of perfect coloured spheres, glowing like pearls that burned from within.

'They are our Rulers,' Karl's voice said, 'and this is our world. Lost people locked up forever in a dead ball of cold rock with the remains of a sun to warm

123

us. Is it any wonder that we break out from time to time?'

Jonathan felt his body grow warm, saw the air bloom into a dazzling blue, and was aware once more of his bed, his room, the window and the sun outside stretching to mid-morning.

Now the call came again. Jonathan left the house and looked cautiously up and down the main road. There was no one near. Further up the road he could see a police car parked outside the school gates, but there were no people moving about. He darted across the road and had begun walking up Church Street towards the Smiths' house when he felt himself being pushed in a new direction.

Although he did not know it, he retraced the steps Frank had taken days before, through the grounds of the vacant holiday cottage, across the empty ground and into the bush beyond. He circled round behind the Smiths' house and paused when he reached the back fence.

This time there were no alarms. Jonathan looked at the house standing quiet in the morning sun with no sign of life.

Then Karl was there by the corner of the old cottage. He beckoned and Jonathan hurried across the lawn to the rear of the old building.

'I am sorry to bring you the long way around,' said Karl. 'We wanted you to come unobserved.'

'We?' said Jonathan.

Karl stood aside and Visha stepped forward. 'I wished to see you. I have seen you before but we have not really spoken. I am Visha.'

'And from now on you had better call me Garl.'

'Garl?'

'That is my real name.'

'Why does your mother wish to see me?'

'Visha is not my mother,' said Garl. 'We had to look like mother and son, so we acted the part. We do things differently on our world. I think I showed you enough to make you see that. We are two members of the same race, but that is all.'

'But you are a child, like me,' said Jonathan.

Garl shook his head. 'Being young or old does not mean much to us. What the mind holds is what counts. Our race would never have survived if we had been forced to waste time waiting for people to grow up. None of us has had a childhood.'

'You must have a mother and father.'

'I was born, of course, as we all are, but to which two people I have no idea. It is of no concern to us.'

Visha looked around. 'I think we should go inside. There is not much time and it is best that we should not be seen together.'

Garl led the way. Old blankets had been draped over the windows of the dusty junk room and a new light bulb of low power hung from a flex. The piles of old furniture had been rearranged. The far corner of the room had been cleaned. A table stood near the bed and on it were mugs, plates and a loaf of bread.

Jonathan gaped in astonishment. Myra lay on the bed, her face still vacant looking, but registering Jonathan's arrival with a faint smile. Alongside the bed was an old armchair. Frank was sitting in it, his wrists tied securely to the wooden arms, and a look of fury and frustration on his face. His mouth was gagged with a wide strip of sticking plaster.

Garl touched Jonathan's elbow. 'I said a few days ago that I would explain everything, and I will, but the explanation is not the one I thought I would give. We haven't much time. Come into the house.'

'But don't you know that people are looking for them all over Wilkes Beach?' Jonathan gasped.

'Of course we know,' said Visha. 'It is not our doing that they are here. Do as Garl requests please. Come inside. It is time you knew. In fact it is almost too late.'

# X

# FIRST EXPEDITION

'He knew she was here,' said Visha.

Garl led Jonathan into the living room and showed him to a chair. 'The front door was unlocked, otherwise I'm sure he would have forced his way through it.'

'You mean he just barged in here?' Jonathan asked.

'If "barged" means something like "charged", then yes, that's exactly what he did,' Garl replied.

Visha sat down opposite Jonathan. 'To put it simply, Mr Gibbons arrived here late last night. He walked in and demanded to know the whereabouts of Mrs Gibbons.'

Garl grinned. 'What he actually said was, "My friends, I am very tired and very worried, and if you don't lead me to Myra right now I will forget that I am a gentleman and do something painful to you".'

'What did you do?'

'We led him out the back and showed him Myra — and then Visha put him to sleep for a little while,' Garl said.

'Then we tied him to the chair,' Visha added.

'But what was Myra doing here in the first place? Did you kidnap her or something?'

They told him how she had arrived and how they had discovered her.

'But why did she come here?' Jonathan said.

'She cannot tell us,' said Visha. 'She has been in a kind of trance since Garl found her sitting on that old bed. We cannot penetrate her mind. Her thoughts are a maze of strange memories and ideas. But we have deduced the reasons and come to the only possible explanation.'

Jonathan was bewildered. 'I don't understand why you have brought me here. I cannot . . . '

Garl interrupted. 'You will understand nothing until you know much more, about us and about this house. That's why I brought you here and I think it best that you save your questions until you have read this.'

He passed Jonathan a small folder containing several handwritten pages. 'These are the main points of the instructions given to Visha and me before we departed on this expedition. Of course, we did not receive them ourselves in this way. I have written them down in the form of a report which I hope will impress you, even if you find parts of it difficult to understand.'

'You want me to read this now?'

'Yes please,' said Visha. 'As Garl says, nothing will make sense until you do. We will leave you alone.'

When they had left the room, Jonathan opened the folder and began reading the first piece of paper. He turned the pages that Garl had laboriously written, amazed at what he read. He noticed, too, the growth from the child-like printing of the opening sections to the bold, assured written script of the final pages. The opening words of the last section were embellished and ornamented with swirls and flourishes that reminded him of a medieval manuscript.

4. *Tasks to be Carried Out by the Second Close Contact Expedition*

4.1 *Attempt to discover the identities of those human beings on whom the genetic transplant operations were performed and, if they are still living, to find out if any changes have taken place in their mental abilities.*

4.2 *If this is not possible, you are instructed to observe the inhabitants of the community with the aim of detecting any sign of the ability to use thought transfer as a means of communication.*

4.3 *If any such human is located, you are to trace his or her line of descent through three generations and work out the chances of a parent, grandparent or great-grandparent being one of the specimens used by the First Contact Expedition.*

4.4 *We are unable to instruct you on how you should act if your search is successful. It is vital that no further harm should come to the native inhabitants. But if the unauthorized experiments carried out by the First Contact Expedition have, in fact, succeeded in producing a mutation in the human brain, it could well be advisable to make contact with any people affected and inform them of the facts. Tell them what happened if you think it the most sensible course of action.*

Jonathan closed the folder. It was like the insurance policies or business papers he had seen from time to time, left lying on the dining table at home after the mail had been opened. The language belonged to offices with panelled walls, and serious looking men wearing dark suits and horn-rimmed spectacles.

'I thought it would be fun to write it like that.'

Jonathan jumped at the sound of Garl's voice behind him. 'I don't understand parts of it.'

'I know, but you will when you grow older, and we will try to explain what you find confusing.'

129

'What do you mean, "when I grow older"?'

'The folder is yours to keep forever,' said Garl. 'You have been entrusted with a secret. What you do with it when you are grown up and fully understand what it means will be up to you.'

'A secret? For me alone?'

Garl shook his head slowly. 'No, not completely yours. There is someone else who has a right to know some of the truth — two people in fact.' He smiled at Jonathan's blank look. 'Can't you guess? Look at the last page again. We are to find someone who can communicate by projecting thought patterns — or someone who can receive and respond to them.'

'But doesn't that mean me?' Jonathan whispered. His face was pale. 'I can do that. Does that mean that something has happened to me? Do you mean you've done something to my brain?'

His voice rose to a shout and he grabbed Garl's arm and shook him. 'It does, doesn't it? I'm the one you tampered with! Ever since that first dream! What have you done to me?'

Jonathan was working himself into a state of hysteria. Garl said nothing but calmed and gentled Jonathan's mind as it plunged and kicked. When he had quietened, Jonathan released Garl's arm and slumped back into the chair.

'You have forgotten what comes later on the page,' said Garl. 'We were to work out the chances of a parent or grandparent being one of the specimens, one of the people whose brain was interfered with.'

Jonathan's eyes brightened, 'And you checked?'

'Of course. You see, I must admit that we thought you were the one, or one of several. You are

130

remarkable. You have a gift that has lain dormant since you were born, but already in this short space of time you have learned to use it in a way that is astounding. I was certain that you were a descendant of those poor people who were used in the experiment conducted by that madman.'

'Madman? You mean the leader of that first expedition?'

'I do. He was mad, deranged. He put his own curiosity, his own self-interest above the good of others — he thought he was a god. Gods have their uses, but they must never be visible. If you see someone who claims to be a god, then you are looking at a fraud. Now he is dead, and so are the human beings he played with. They died because of him.'

'But you said you were told to find someone,' said Jonathan slowly, 'and you admitted — almost anyway — that you've been successful. You've said that it isn't me.'

'That is correct. Your parents and grandparents were not here at the right time. Visha checked in the records at the court house. She told me on that day I fell over the cliff. Remember? We met her on the path. That is when Visha first saw you.'

'Then who is it?'

'She is lying on the bed in the outside room.'

'You mean Myra? Mrs Gibbons?'

Garl nodded. 'That is who I mean.'

'But how could she be the one? How could you know that?'

'The evidence tells us,' said Garl.

'What evidence?'

'We will tell you, but I said that other people had

a right to know. Myra is the innocent victim. She must be told. But she will not fully understand because she is confused and her past is a chaotic memory of things that happened to other people. Frank must know as well, to protect her when we have gone. He above all must be made to understand.'

'When you have gone? Are you leaving? When are you leaving?'

'More of that later. We're returning to the outside room. The two of us — Visha and I — are going to talk to Frank about some of the things you know already, from what you've just read. Frank is going to listen. He is a clever man. He will listen and learn, and after that we hope that he will be contented. We suspect he has guessed a lot already. He has been prowling about, around this house and up in the hills.'

'And if he's not contented? You have him tied and gagged. I suppose he's angry.'

'Of course. He thinks we are responsible for Myra's distress and he is furious. If we do not succeed it will be up to you — after we have gone. I hope there will be no need. But for now we will let Frank think you know little more than he does. Just pretend that you're hearing everything for the first time.'

Jonathan followed Garl from the house, round the path and in through the rear door to the old room. Little had changed since he had left it shortly before, except that Visha had pulled around some old furniture and brought out more food and drink.

Visha nodded Jonathan towards a stool. 'We thought we would have morning tea while we chatted. Please sit.'

She passed a mug to Myra who slowly accepted

132

it with a shy smile. Frank moved his jaw muscles behind his gag. He glared at Jonathan as though he had found a new enemy. Jonathan hoped desperately that whatever was going to be discussed would turn out well. Sitting near Frank, he felt like a traitor watching a friend being kept in prison.

They settled in their chairs. Visha turned to Jonathan. 'We have brought you here as a witness. Do you understand?'

'I think so,' Jonathan said.

'I am going to speak to Mr Gibbons. I want you to listen. I want you to know in case Mr Gibbons forgets what I am going to tell him. We have chosen you to be a witness because you are young and your mind is not cluttered with silly ideas.'

Jonathan picked up Garl's thought. 'You want me to listen and remember,' he said.

'I'm glad you understand,' Visha replied. 'Garl said you were a bright boy.'

Jonathan almost smiled but stopped himself in time. Visha began talking in clear, precise tones, without pausing, keeping her eyes fixed on Frank's face.

'Almost sixty years ago, four members of our race came out of the sky and landed in the clearing you visited several days ago.'

Frank's eyes flickered. Visha had his full attention.

'Why they came here does not concern you. What they did while they were here is very much your concern. They committed a great wrong which affected your wife, Myra. I am here to apologize most deeply for their crime and to tell you what happened.

'At that time a house stood near here that has since burned down. You can still see the remains of its

133

foundations on the waste ground at the back, near the bushline. I see by your eyes that you know the place I mean. It is almost certain that the four of whom I speak lived in that house.'

Visha looked around the room. 'At that time this house was no more than this old building. A family lived here. Their names were Edward Sorensen and Thelma Sorensen — the parents — and two children, Charles and Jean. Their third child, Myra, was as yet unborn. An experiment was carried out on those four human beings — parents and two children. I would guess that they had no knowledge of it. The people of my race have an ability to induce sleep in others, as you well know.'

Here, Visha stared at Frank, who was looking intently at the small group around the table.

'I can see that you are interested,' said Visha. 'I would be willing to remove the gag from your mouth in return for your promise to remain silent.'

Frank nodded. Garl moved behind him and removed the tape from his face. Then he untied the ropes that held Frank's arms to the chair. Thankfully he slumped back, flexing his wrists and moving his jaws from side to side. He stretched out an arm and took Myra's hand. She continued to sit quietly at the head of the bed. At the mention of the name 'Sorensen', then her own name, her eyes had brightened suddenly, and now she waited for Visha to continue.

'The experiment was probably performed in this room. The operation took the form of a transplant. It was almost certainly the leader of the expedition who was the donor. From his brain cells there was removed a minute quantity of a substance which your

134

scientists call deoxyribonucleic acid, or DNA. They do not know its structure yet, but they are close to discovering it.

'It was made into a chemical compound by a process known to us. This substance was then injected into the brain of each member of the Sorensen family, at a position about here.' She pointed to a spot midway between the top of her ear and her eyebrow. 'The transplanted DNA became part of the DNA that belonged naturally to the host brain, like a new piece of thread being spliced into an existing one.

'And what did this new segment contain? It held genes, and genes are what determine the characteristics living things inherit from their parents — the colour of hair and eyes, the shape of the nose, and so on. The people of our race are different from human beings in one important way. Our brains have evolved so that we can use our minds much more widely than you can — or so we thought.

'The leader of our group decided to put things right. He took it upon himself to introduce into the brains of his four specimens the genes that would enable their brains to behave as ours do. Having done this, he and the other members of the expedition departed. They recorded what they had done but unfortunately, because of a mishap which we need not discuss now, the records were destroyed. Until now we have not known what really happened. We were sent to find out. Now we know.'

Frank leaned forward in his chair. He moistened his lips and when he spoke his voice was hoarse. 'Myra's family died within three months of each other didn't they?'

'Yes, they died and they are buried alongside each other in the graveyard.'

'Why did they die?'

'Almost certainly because of what was done to them. In time, the segment transplanted into their brains must have produced something toxic — something that poisoned their brain cells and killed them. Or perhaps an alien virus was introduced in the transplant that eventually proved lethal because their bodies' immune systems could not cope with it. We do not know. But it can be no coincidence that they died within weeks of each other.'

Jonathan had been following Visha's words closely, but now he turned to Myra. Visha followed his puzzled gaze. 'Myra was not born when the experiment was done,' she said. 'Her family did not die at once. There was time for Myra to be born and live to five years of age before she was orphaned.'

'So the operation didn't affect her,' Jonathan said. 'It couldn't have if she wasn't born.'

'There you are wrong,' said Garl. 'We are almost sure it did affect her, and now we are going to discover if our suspicions are correct.'

He nodded to Visha who took from her pocket the small box she always carried with her. Garl and Visha watched Myra closely. She noticed the box, then her attention wandered as she became aware of all eyes upon her. She smiled, as though trying to please. Visha opened the box. She removed the globe of small crystal spheres and held it up so that the light bulb above reflected faintly in its clear, rounded surfaces.

Instantly Myra's face breathed life and she leaned forward with a gasp. She stared at the beautiful object and stretched out hesitantly as Visha lowered it into her lap. Still watching Myra, she passed her fingers over the surface of the globe. As the colours began to glow within it and swirl in rainbow pools, there passed into Myra's face a look of pure joy and triumph.

Again she reached out, but Garl shook his head. 'Not yet Mrs Gibbons, but in a moment, I promise you.'

Visha turned to Jonathan, offering him the globe. 'Would you please try to do as I did.'

Jonathan concentrated on the cluster of spheres but could produce no change. The only colour came from the reflection of the light bulb glimmering on the surface. He was about to return it to Visha when Garl pointed to Frank. Jonathan passed the globe to him and they watched as Frank stared at it, looking embarrassed.

'I wouldn't know how to begin,' he said at last.

'Garl and I are both able to make the colours dance,' said Visha. 'It is second nature to us. We were born with the skill, as are all members of our race.' She looked across to the corner of the room. 'Now give the globe to Myra,' she said softly.

Myra reached out eagerly like someone being presented with a rare and precious jewel and took the object, her hands fumbling in their haste. Almost as soon as her fingers closed around it, pale colours swept up from within, growing stronger until each tiny sphere glowed and the whole orb was like all the suns of the universe, living, dying and almost dead, nestling against each other.

'That is the vision of the universe lodged deep in the minds of the people of our race,' said Visha. 'Myra has inherited something from her parents that was planted in their minds without their knowledge — something that destroyed them, but which was passed to her in some distorted form, cleansed of its danger, when she was conceived.' She looked at Frank. 'Do you understand what I am saying?'

'I think so. The alien genes, or some of them anyway, were passed to Myra from her parents and they became part of her.' Visha was about to speak but Frank held up his hand and continued. 'She could never understand the impulse inside her. She felt a need to do something to satisfy it, so she was drawn to the graves of her family. But that still wasn't enough. So she spread her coloured stones on the table cloth and pushed them into shapes. It was the nearest she could reach — to that.' He turned to the glowing orb resting in Myra's hands.

'You have great insight,' said Visha.

'I'm not stupid, if that's what you mean,' Frank said, 'and remember that I've known my wife much longer than you have. I've had time to think.'

Myra's whole being was absorbed in the colours that she was now beginning to move in lilting rhythms over the surface of the spheres, her face lighting up in delight as she discovered new patterns. Then she looked up, straight at Visha, and her face began to crumple. Hesitantly, she passed the globe back to her, allowing its colours to wash away.

But Visha shook her head very deliberately. 'It is yours,' she said. 'It is yours for as long as you live. It is our gift to you. I am only sorry that we can give you nothing more.'

Myra drew the globe back towards her, holding

it against her body as though it were a lost child. When the others left the room she was leaning against Frank's shoulder, as serene and tranquil as a rising moon.

Visha locked the door behind them and they returned to the house.

'How did you know?' Jonathan asked.

'I finally guessed when I saw the stones lying on the grass,' said Garl. 'Ask Belinda and Susan to tell you about it.'

'And then Myra came to us,' Visha said .'From the time we arrived she has been drawn to this place, and at last the urge became too strong. Do not ask me to explain how, but in some strange way the wild thread in her mind was drawn to us like metal to a magnet. Our minds must have seemed like a lost home. Now she is contented. We have given her something to hold on to us by and I think we can leave safely and no longer harm her.'

'When you leave?' said Jonathan sharply. He looked at Garl. 'You said that before. Must you leave now?'

'Enough people know about us already,' said Garl, 'and we cannot risk being discovered by those who are searching for Frank and Myra. We cannot become further involved. Besides, we have completed our task. We have discovered what we were sent to find out.'

'When will you leave?' Jonathan asked quietly.

'Tonight. There is no alternative. We must leave tonight.'

Jonathan blinked rapidly, his eyes beginning to glisten. He turned towards the door.

'Wait,' said Garl. 'We cannot go without your help.'

'What do you mean?'

'Frank and Myra must be kept here until after we are safely out of the way. We will need someone to release them,' said Garl.

'There is something else,' Visha added. 'We need to know what is happening outside. We can sense much activity but we need to find out what searches are planned for today. You could do this for us. Question your parents. Will you return this afternoon? We need your help.'

Jonathan nodded. 'You can read my answer can't you?'

Garl grinned. 'Of course we can. Thank you for being so willing.' His grin grew broader and he almost laughed.

'What's so funny?' Jonathan asked.

'I'm sorry,' Garl said. 'I wasn't laughing at you. I was thinking about the whole situation. It is very amusing in a cruel kind of way. Yes, that's the way to describe it — a cruel joke, with Myra's family the victims and Myra herself a strange, deluded orphan.'

'What he means,' said Visha, 'is that all this — the experiment, the transplant, the anguish that followed — all this was completely unnecessary. You are what those four who came before us were trying to produce.'

'That's what is so funny and so cruel.' Garl said. 'There was no need to interfere, no need to tamper. You are just like us. You were here all the time, and there must be others like you. All that was needed was someone to trigger you. Someone to give a sleeping part of your brain a little nudge. And that someone was me. It's so funny it's enough to make you weep.'

He turned quickly and left the room.

# XI

## DEPARTURE

Jonathan's return home was like an entrance upon a stage full of actors, all impatiently awaiting his arrival. Belinda and Susan were on the floor helping Mary build a house with blocks. Mrs Wilkes was whisking plates from the table. Mr Wilkes was hastily gulping the last of his cup of tea.

'Jonathan! Where have you been? We've finished lunch.'

'I didn't realize it was so late,' Jonathan said, taking in the bustle around him, wondering why Belinda and Susan were on the scene, and carefully avoiding the question his mother had asked him. As he suspected, she was in too much of a hurry to notice he hadn't answered.

'Never mind, you're here now. I've got to return to the shop this afternoon, but I'm not taking Mary. She's bored down there. I was going to hand her over to you, but you weren't around. But then Belinda and Susan came looking for you and they said they wouldn't mind looking after her until you arrived. You're here now, so you can take over. All right?'

She finished in a breathless rush, dumping the remaining dishes in the sink. 'You can get your own lunch, then wash these later. I've got to go.'

'What's Dad doing this afternoon?' Jonathan asked, as his mother disappeared through the door.

'Ask him!' she shouted over her shoulder. 'I've got to zoom!' Then she was gone.

'Dad, where are you . . . '

'I heard you,' his father said, as he pulled on his jacket. 'We're starting a house-to-house search this afternoon.'

Jonathan's stomach suddenly felt like coiling tentacles. He hoped his face had not turned pale.

'All the houses?' he asked, in a voice that croaked and which he managed to turn into a coughing fit. 'All the houses?' he repeated as calmly as he could.

His father glanced at him curiously. 'No, the empty baches and holiday houses first. We're checking to see that they're secure and no one has broken in. Why?'

'Oh, I just wondered,' said Jonathan. 'Can I help?'

'You've got to look after Mary.'

'I forgot. Where are you going to start?'

'Start what?'

'The search.'

'I think they plan to start with the empty houses around here and then work out. In fact, I'm going to look at that place of ours at the top of Church Street before I go back to school.'

The tentacles in Jonathan's stomach turned to ice. He almost shouted to his father as he opened the door. 'But Karl lives there!'

'What?'

'The Smiths live there. Remember?'

His father turned back with a laugh. 'Do you know, I'd completely forgotten. Thanks for reminding me. See you later.'

Jonathan leaned back against the kitchen bench and breathed in deeply. He could feel his heart beating.

He tried to be casual as he walked through from the kitchen to the main room. Belinda and Susan looked up as he entered.

'What's the matter? You look as if you've had a fright,' Belinda said.

'It's nothing,' said Jonathan. 'I ran out of breath running home.'

'Well, I suppose we might as well go,' said Susan, standing up.

'No, you help me,' said Mary.

'Jonathan's here now.'

'No, I want you.'

'Why?'

'Because you make better houses.'

Jonathan felt a surge of relief as he saw his afternoon begin to look less bleak than he had imagined. But the moment was brief.

'Jonathan will be in charge, and you'll help him look after me,' Mary announced firmly.

'What about me?' Belinda asked.

'You'll be the second helper,' Mary said at once.

'Why can't I be in charge?'

'Because Jonathan's my brother, aren't you Jonathan?'

She turned her wide, innocent eyes towards him and he knew at once that she had unknowingly pinned him to a wall he could not escape from. Mary was his sister and he was her brother and this was one of those times when you couldn't play Pass the Parcel — not because his parents stood in the background to deal out justice, but because of something deeper. He saw the funny side of it. Genes, he thought to himself, have a lot to answer for, and before today I hardly knew they existed.

'Yes Mary, I'm your brother, no doubt about it. I won't be long.'

Going to the kitchen, Jonathan prepared a few sandwiches and slowly munched them as he ran hot water into the sink. Then he deliberately filled his mind with images of what he had learned from his father, hoping that Garl would detect them. Waiting in the house, Visha and Garl would be alert for sensations and signals from the world around them and he was confident that his message would get through. He wondered if his feelings would go with the images — a feeling that he would not see Garl again, a sense of sadness and regret.

Almost at once images forced their way into his own mind: a key and a door, then the darkness of a star-filled sky. He knew what they meant.

When he had finished drying the dishes Jonathan returned to the living room. 'What shall we do?'

'Go to the beach,' responded Mary instantly.

'We always go to the beach,' said Jonathan.

'I'm the one who's being looked after, and I want to go to the beach!'

'All right, all right,' Jonathan said. 'Do you two want to come? You don't have to.'

'Who could resist an invitation like that,' said Belinda. 'Of course we'll come. There's nothing else to do anyway. I'll be glad to get back to school.'

Walking down the road to the beach, the two girls stared intently at the Gibbons' cottage as they passed the gate. Jonathan was almost too embarrassed to look.

'Myra's gone away,' Mary said.

'Who told you that?' Jonathan asked.

'Mummy. I wanted to go over and see her, but Mummy said she'd gone for a holiday. Where has she gone to?'

'I don't know,' Jonathan said.

'Didn't she tell you?'

'No.'

'Why not?'

'Because it's a secret.'

Mary understood secrets. She slipped her hand into Jonathan's and concentrated on trying to stand on his shadow as it bobbed and wavered in front of them.

'Have you seen Paul today?' Susan asked.

'I saw him this morning on his way up to Madsen's farm,' said Belinda. 'He said he was going to cut thistles, but I wouldn't mind betting he'll take the chance to have a look around the back paddocks and the bush.'

'He's taken it to heart, hasn't he?'

'Myra going missing you mean?' said Jonathan. 'He feels he's partly to blame. He thinks he should have kept watch on her while Frank was away.'

'Well, I hope they find her soon,' said Belinda. 'You know, I can't help thinking Frank has found her.'

'Why?' asked Jonathan sharply.

'Because he's missing too. I think he's with her. I think he knew where to look. That's my guess anyway, and I think it's as good as anyone else's.'

Jonathan pretended to be looking at seagulls, then ran ahead with Mary across the dunes towards the beach. Dried seed pods on the lupins rattled in a wind that was beginning to sweep up from the south-west. Winter was coming. For several days this breeze had

145

been growing stronger. The sea was losing its summer colour as a cold, grey sheen slid over its surface and the offshore wind whipped tiny manes of spray from the waves.

They walked across the soft sand above the tide line, dried seaweed crackling under their feet. Mary began looking for crabs at once and was not happy until they had reached the hard-packed sand further down where the sea swept twice a day. Towards the northern end of the beach Aaron Clark's boat was bumping across the waves, spray flying high from the bows as the wind picked it up.

'I'm going down to see what he's caught,' said Jonathan. He ran down to the wet sand and trotted along the beach. Soft sand blown in sheets from further up stung his legs and ankles. By the time Jonathan reached the boat, Aaron had pulled it up out of the inshore breakers and was leaning against the bow resting, looking up at the skyline.

'Did you catch anything?' Jonathan asked, as he panted to a halt.

'I wasn't trying too hard,' Aaron replied. 'I was having another search along the coastline. But I put out some lines on the way back and didn't catch a single thing. Not even a crab. You know what that means don't you?'

'Put away the boat for winter,' said Jonathan with a grin.

'Absolutely right. Cold weather is on the way and it's time for me to catch up on my reading.'

Aaron continued to squint towards the horizon. 'Looks like a black eye doesn't it?'

'What does?'

Aaron pointed. 'You see that depression in the hills? When the sun starts to go down it casts a shadow across it. Makes it look like a black eye.'

'I suppose it does,' Jonathan said.

'You know, if Frank doesn't show up soon, I think we could do worse than have a look up there.'

'Why?'

'Eh? Oh nothing. I was just talking to myself. Do you want to give me a push?'

Jonathan helped move the boat clear of the wet sand that might suck down the trailer wheels, then left Aaron to bed down the boat for winter, as he put it. He strolled back up the beach, hunching his shoulders against the chill wind, wishing he had brought a jersey. Mary would be cold. He doubted if this expedition to the beach would last much longer.

But when he reached her, Mary was engrossed in creating a figure drawn in the sand. She was scampering back and forth searching for shells, directing Belinda and Susan as they helped her.

Susan called as he came within earshot. 'Come and look at what Mary's done. It's the strangest thing.'

Mary had reached the age where her efforts to draw the human figure were beginning to produce shapes recognizable to someone other than herself. In the hard sand she had drawn a stick figure seated on some unknown object, but it was clearly a woman because lines of long hair were scored into the sand. The round head smiled like a new moon. The hands, at the end of impossibly long arms, had several fingers splayed out in a rigid fan, and they rested on the figure's knees. Between them Mary was slowly adding to a cluster of shells that she was carefully embedding in the sand.

'What is it?' Jonathan said.

'Ask her,' said Belinda quietly.

'What have you drawn, Mary?' Jonathan asked, kneeling beside her.

'Well!' said Mary. 'That's Myra.' She looked at Jonathan to make sure he had understood. 'And she's sitting down. And she's holding something shiny. And she's looking at it. And that's what's on her knees. See?'

A ghost appearing in broad daylight could not have startled Jonathan more. He looked at Mary, darting back and forth as she added shells to the shape she had created, and tried to understand what was happening under the bouncing hair, deep within her mind. Of one thing he was certain — Mary herself had no idea that she was doing anything unusual.

'Where is Frank?' Belinda asked casually.

'He's beside her sometimes,' said Mary, 'but I haven't got time to put him in because he keeps going away and walking around.'

'Where does he go to?'

'I don't know. But he's beside her sometimes.'

Jonathan concentrated on keeping his voice low and natural. 'Where are they Mary?'

Mary had gone on a more extended walk for a shell she had spied along the beach. She was becoming impatient.

'I told you! Myra's sitting down and Frank is there sometimes.'

'Where is Myra sitting down?' Susan asked.

By now Mary was exasperated. 'Up there!' she said sharply. She pointed in a direction that could have meant the sky, the hills or anywhere except the beach.

'I want to go home Jonathan. Take me home, I'm cold.'

'All right, we'll go home,' Jonathan said. He winked at Susan and Belinda. 'She has quite an imagination hasn't she?'

'Either that, or second sight,' said Belinda. 'Wouldn't it be wonderful if she turned out to be a baby witch?'

'No, it would not,' Jonathan replied. 'I'd get the blame!' He took Mary's hand. 'Shall we go home and make popcorn?'

Mary agreed at once, as Jonathan knew she would, and he lost no time in saying goodbye to Belinda and Susan, hoping they would not want to come as well. Fortunately, they had other plans. He looked down at his sister's small head as they strolled home and was tempted to read what was going on inside it. Then he remembered the promise he had made to himself and resisted the temptation to penetrate her thoughts again. She would know it, and last time he had come close to frightening her. He held her hand tightly and hurried home, knowing that he would have to wait patiently for the night before he did anything else.

Jonathan lay in bed and waited. He pulled back the curtains and watched the sky. There was no moon and the brightest stars seemed to pulse with light against the blackness, their clarity blurred and softened by the invisible atmosphere around the Earth. He tried counting the stars visible in one square of the window. Each time he thought he had the total, he noticed another faint speck of light he had overlooked. He gave up and watched the blackness instead. It was much more relaxing.

With a start he snatched himself back from sleep and forced himself awake. That had been close. He could hear the radio playing in the other room. He looked at his bedside clock. It was half-past-ten. How long would his parents listen? He hoped it was a boring programme. He recited all his multiplication tables frontwards and backwards, then looked at the clock again. Ten minutes had passed. Should he try turning on his bedside light and reading? Too risky.

It was after eleven o'clock before the drone of the radio suddenly stopped. Jonathan turned over quickly, pulling the blankets around him, and settled into a steady breathing pattern that, he hoped, would sound like someone asleep. He concentrated on stopping his eyelids blinking. He heard his mother come through the door and move to his bedside, sensing her leaning over him. She left the room and Jonathan relaxed.

How long would they take to get to sleep? He waited for fifteen minutes before tip-toeing to the bedroom door and gently easing it open. Silence. No sign of any lights. He stood absolutely still listening to the quietness of the house. He would have to go now. Already the hands on the clock were moving towards midnight. He dressed quickly and considered how he would leave the house. Door or window? If he used the back door the hinges would squeak. The front door lock would click loudly when he closed it from the outside. Besides, any noise he might make scrambling through a window would be shielded by his bedroom door.

Standing on his bed he lifted the latch of the window

150

directly above and gently pushed it out. He raised one knee on to the sill, then hauled himself up until he was kneeling on it. He had never realized how awkward it was to climb out of a window. Actors in films never seemed to have any problems. He squirmed around until he could sit on the sill with his legs dangling outside. Giving himself a push, he jumped. As soon as he was in mid-air he remembered that the window he had chosen was directly above a huge hydrangea bush that grew like a flowering puffball below. A split second later he was part of it, with branches crackling and snapping like fireworks on bonfire night.

Jonathan lay absolutely still waiting for the lights to come on. The noise had seemed deafening. Nothing happened. Slowly he extracted himself from the shattered bush, wondering if he would be able to blame the mess on fighting cats. He doubted it. Time enough to worry about it later. He found an old garden stake and gently pushed the window shut as far as it would go. Luckily the afternoon wind had died away and there was nothing to blow it open again.

Jonathan ran around the corner of the house, almost winded himself on the closed gate, then walked quickly up the road, beathing hard. He paused for a moment to collect his thoughts. The village was quiet. No lights showed anywhere. Above him he could make out the jet blackness of the hills against the glowing darkness of the sky. As his eyes became adjusted to the faint starlight he found he could see a surprising distance. Once his panic had subsided he felt the night around him grow gentle and solemn.

Jonathan hurried up Church Street and slipped

through the gate at the end. He stopped. The house was completely dark. He moved around to the back door.

'Garl.'

He called again, a little louder. 'Garl!'

There was no sound. He tapped at the door, then knocked firmly and waited. No one answered. He stretched out his hand and carefully turned the knob. The door was unlocked and with the pressure of his hand it slowly opened.

Jonathan moved on to the step and peered into the darkness. There was no sign of life. He could hear nothing.

'Garl, are you there?'

No answer. He could hear a clock ticking in another room. Jonathan eased his way inside. He could see nothing. He felt around the edge of the door frame and his fingers groped against a switch. He poised his fingers over it then, holding his breath, turned it on. The kitchen flared with light. In the sudden glare Jonathan had time to notice a torch on the bench a few steps from him. Then he switched off the light.

His eyes swirled and swam with the after images. When the confusion had died down and his vision had readjusted itself, he edged forward to the bench and felt carefully for the torch. His hand bumped against it. Pointing it to the floor, he switched on. The batteries were low and the bulb gave off a dim, orange light. He moved quickly to the next room and flashed the beam around the walls. The room was empty. Jonathan's heart was thudding. He walked through to a bedroom. There was no one there. They had gone.

Retracing his steps he moved back to the kitchen.

Lying on the bench was a brown folder. On the cover were written the words, 'You forgot this. Make sure you keep it safe.' Beside the folder lay a key, and alongside that an envelope with his name on it. He placed the envelope inside the folder then slid it under his jersey. Then he took the key and opened the back door. The torch suddenly died as the batteries gave out. He felt his way around the path to the door of the outside room.

Reaching the entrance, Jonathan held the key in one hand and felt carefully for the lock. He located the small opening, then pressed his fingers firmly against the door as he prepared to guide the end of the key. But at the first hint of pressure the door swung slowly inward, the bottom scraping on the concrete where it did not quite clear the floor. The door was unlocked.

Jonathan's heart thumped. He listened, but there was no sound from inside. All he could see was a rectangle of blackness. He felt for the light switch, and in the same instant he felt himself being hurried, hastened, to go at once, to go to the beach. Confused, he switched on the light and stepped inside. He took in the bed, the table, the chairs, just as he had seen them that morning. But there was no one there. Myra and Frank had gone.

He turned off the light, pulled the door shut and leaned against it, trying to think clearly. Through his bewilderment came that strong call, clear and insistent, pulling him towards the beach. He knew it could come from only one source. He was being commanded and there was no resisting it.

He ran. He ran back down Church Street, past his own home, towards the beach. Out of the corner of his eye he noticed a light shining in a window of the Gibbons' cottage, but even this, startling as it was, did not stop him.

The beach at night looked like a pale, ghostly avenue stretching to darkness in either direction. Streamers of white foam grew and faded in the blackness as the breakers curled and crashed in a steady, growling rumble. Jonathan ran to the edge of the soft sand and sat down to wait. He felt very tired. He hugged his knees and dug in the sand with his toes. Time passed very slowly and he could feel himself growing drowsy.

Suddenly he felt alert. His head was tugged and adjusted until he was staring at the invisible black eye of the basin far up in the hills. Then the darkness was lit by a pale, white glow. The light stayed still for a few minutes, then brightened and began to rise slowly.

As it reached the level of the hilltops the glowing disc swept around in an enormous arc, gliding over the houses towards the sea. Not a sound came from it, yet Jonathan felt, rather than heard, a strange humming, as though all the air around him was vibrating. He watched, his neck craned back, as the disc passed over him. He was sure it tilted in a kind of salute before moving swiftly out over the ocean. Then it darted upwards at a steep angle — an arrow of light that dwindled in seconds to a speck before disappearing into the black void.

Jonathan's feet took command and led him towards home, and just as surely took him through the gate to the Gibbons' cottage as he was about to walk past it. The light still shone in the kitchen window. He went to the back door and was about to knock when it opened. Frank stood there, smiling.

He reached out and ruffled Jonathan's hair. 'We were expecting you. Come in.'

Myra was sitting at the dining table, sipping a cup of tea, her back erect and her eyes alert. 'You're up late tonight Jonathan,' she said, 'but I suppose you have an excuse. Come and sit beside me.'

Jonathan eased carefully into the chair beside her. She brushed some sand from his face. 'You must have had a good view from the beach. I felt them pass overhead. And now they've gone forever. At least I shall never see them again. I'm glad they came back. I'm contented now. But I'm forgetting my manners. Would you like a cup of tea? You must be cold.'

Jonathan shook his head, marvelling at the old Myra he saw before him, gentle and self-assured.

'Some cocoa perhaps?'

'Yes please.'

'Frank will fetch it for you. I think I shall go to bed, if you'll excuse me.'

She left the room, walking with great dignity. Jonathan noticed that she carried a small bundle, something wrapped in a deep blue cloth, a soft, old fabric that fell in folds around her arm.

Frank returned quickly with a mug of cocoa which he placed in front of Jonathan. He looked at the boy's apprehensive face and chuckled. 'Don't worry Jonathan. It's all over now, and for the best.'

'How . . . how did you . . .'

'How did we get out? It's a very old lock on that door. I had plenty of time to wander around and have a look. In fact, I could have got out much earlier, but I thought it better to stay put until they had gone. I just paced up and down. I had time to think, you see. Things have been put right. There was no point in making trouble.

'I'll tell the police I found Myra in some old shack in the bush that I took her to once when we were young. I'll say she lost her memory, or something like that, and she was tired and we had to rest a while — I'll think of some story.'

Jonathan tried to speak but Frank held up his hand. 'I don't want to know anything more than I do now. As a matter of fact, I might be able to show you something you don't know about. I'll take you for a walk in the bush on Saturday, up into the hills.'

Jonathan's eyes brightened.

'You can guess where I'm talking about?'

'The basin? The one that looks like a black eye?'

'That's it. They knew I'd been up there. I've a feeling that the boy, Garl, would want you to see it.'

'Garl was my friend — he became my friend,' said Jonathan quietly.

'I could tell that,' said Frank. 'That's why you and I are going to keep our mouths closed. Let your father worry about his tenants disappearing in the middle of the night. Now I think you'd better get home to bed. Have you ever been up this late before?'

Jonathan grinned and shook his head.

He walked slowly home and managed to haul himself up over the window-sill and fall on the bed inside. No one heard him. He hid the brown folder under his clothes in a bottom drawer. His body ached with tiredness but he lay awake for a long time with the curtains pulled back, unable to sleep. He stared at the sky until the stars began to fade, and only as dawn approached did his eyes finally close.

# XII

# SOUVENIRS

Jonathan woke early and read the letter before he was called for breakfast. It was written in Garl's carefully formed handwriting, bold and precise in its strokes without any smudges or blemishes.

*Jonathan Wilkes,*

*I find it strange to think that this is the last time I will make marks like these on a sheet of clean white paper. I am glad things have turned out this way. If we had met this afternoon we would have talked and our words would exist only in our memories until they were forgotten. I could have printed what I want to say on your mind, but then you would probably remember the way I had spoken and forget the message. The truth is, I am entranced with the primitive act of shaping letters and words with a pen held between my fingers. For me it is like performing a lost art, crafting thoughts so that they can be handled on the tongue, kept and used until they are faded by time.*

*When we all talked together today in that old room with Myra and Frank, I kept something from you which you should know and understand. I wonder if you have ever asked yourself why you should suddenly discover powers hidden within your mind. The answer, of course, lies in our presence — Visha and me. You must realize by now that we awakened you, just as we roused and disturbed Myra.*

*Now you must be told what will happen when we have gone. Visha and I have discussed this at length and we are*

*sure that, without our presence, you will go back to what*
*you were. The part of your mind that suddenly stretched itself*
*into life will slowly cramp and sink back into a kind of paralysis.*
*I am telling you this not to be cruel, but so that you will*
*not be disappointed when it happens. If we could have stayed*
*longer we could have trained you, but that was not to be.*

*Look after your sister, Mary, and watch her carefully. I*
*suspect you will have discovered that her mind speaks with*
*a force and clarity that is startling, especially as she seems*
*to be completely unaware of her powers. I have never mentioned*
*this before, but both Visha and I frequently believed that she*
*was one of us. We have eavesdropped on her throughout our*
*stay. We could not help it. There have been times when her*
*dreams have been like raucous screams in our ears. But, as*
*with you, we suspect the dreams will fade.*

*Dreams. For a long time I have wanted to apologize for*
*the first dream I forced into your sleep. I tampered with you.*
*I committed the same sin as the leader of our first expedition.*
*I have often asked myself whether he also felt that irresistible*
*urge I experienced to show my mastery over you. I have*
*sometimes wondered whether I am descended from him because,*
*as I told you once, we do not know our birth mothers and*
*fathers. I have certainly discovered that I am different, and*
*for that I have you to thank. For just as we awakened something*
*in you, you aroused part of me that I did not know existed*
*— you, Paul, Belinda and Susan.*

*What did you bring to life in me? I have no time to analyse*
*it. We are leaving now. But perhaps I can explain by saying*
*that I have a feeling of great sorrow and regret that I will*
*never see you again. That is a sensation I have never before*
*experienced. Perhaps it will fade. I do not really care. At*
*least it happened.*

*You will probably be able to deduce the whereabouts of*

159

*our departure point. Try to visit it when we have gone. I will leave a souvenir. If you cannot find the place, ask Frank Gibbons. As I write this he is pacing up and down the room outside. I think he knows how to escape but wishes to delay the moment until we have departed. He is guarding Myra and will risk nothing where she is concerned. So do not be surprised if the outside room is empty when you go to unlock the door.*

*Visha is calling. I must go. Do not forget to visit the departure point. We will be leaving something of ourselves behind. We have marked it.*

*Garl.*

At breakfast, Jonathan listened quietly as his parents discussed the amazing return of Myra and Frank. The phone seemed to ring incessantly. Just before he left for school, a police constable arrived at the door and he overheard scraps of conversation about huts in the bush and loss of memory. Then there were muttered thanks for his father's help and apologies for 'all the trouble that had been caused'.

Jonathan did not hear as much as he would have liked, because his attention was fixed on the curious, twinkling eyes of Mary. Mary knew! The pictures in Mary's mind did not show a long-forgotten hut in the bush. Her sketches in the sand of the day before were the mere traces of a vision that was held in her mind of Frank pacing a dingy back room and Myra patiently sitting. Jonathan sensed that if she were pushed she could go to that room with absolute certainty and confidence.

Every time Mary opened her mouth, Jonathan feared that she would blurt out the truth. She teased him.

'Mummy, could I have the jam please?'

'Daddy, I want the honey instead.'

'I wonder if Frank and Myra — like honey.'

Jonathan desperately willed her to stay quiet. He glared at her. He thought of kicking her under the table.

Then, finally, when their father and mother had left the room briefly, she released her brother from his torment. She smiled at him gleefully like a conspirator in a plot and winked at him. Jonathan covered his confusion by concentrating on buttering a slice of toast. What was his young sister? He recalled Belinda's comment about a 'baby witch'. He wondered how many 'Marys' in the past had been branded and burned for displaying a rare and natural gift that had suddenly sprung into the open from some hidden cranny in their minds.

The following Saturday morning was warm. Summer was having one last day to itself before winter came. Frank walked ahead, slowly and deliberately, along a path that was becoming well worn. Morning dew dripped from the upper canopy of branches and the ground warmed with the sweet aroma of decay that always reminded Jonathan of coal — a photograph of a slab of coal with a fossil fern embedded in it, a small illustration in an encyclopedia on a shelf in a school room. At the time he had imagined the ancient forest that had died and sunk beneath the ground, carrying the heat of the sun with it, but leaving this one fern frond as a fingerprint to prove that it had once lived.

They reached the basin soon before midday. Frank

led the way confidently, hastening as they drew nearer. Jonathan toiled behind and was almost trotting when they broke through into the clearing. The flat gravel lawn had become a shallow crater. The gravel had subsided and relaxed, now that it had nothing more to hide. Frank sat against a tree and watched as Jonathan walked slowly around the edge, his feet sliding and slipping whenever he wandered off the firm ground. He was almost back to where he had started when he stopped.

In front of him was a tall tree. Fastened to its trunk was a white square which grew into an envelope as he walked towards it. He reached up, pulled it free and peered inside.

'What have you found?' Frank called.

'Nothing much,' Jonathan said.

He tipped the envelope. Two small tinted discs slid into his hand — two brown lenses. He moved his fingers over their glossy surfaces, then carefully folded them in a handkerchief and put them in his pocket.

'Nothing much, just a souvenir,' he said to himself.

He wondered if Garl would ever need them again. What was it he had said? 'Do not forget to visit the departure point. We have marked it.' What had he meant? Jonathan looked around but could see nothing more. Then he was drawn to the shallow crater. Suppose they had left something hidden below the surface, a fingerprint that no living human would ever see? He slid down the slope, his feet sinking up to his ankles in the fine, dirt gravel. He stood at the bottom.

'Be careful!' Frank said. 'You might sink out of sight in that stuff.'

Jonathan waited. There was nothing to see. Then, as he was about to shuffle back to the edge, he suddenly felt his mind drain and begin to fill with the familiar pale light. Then it faded and there was nothing more. Disappointed, he scrambled back to the rim of the crater. But he was certain something was concealed down there like a guardian or sentry waiting to turn the handle on a door that led from one world to another. Or a beacon ready to guide a messenger not sure of the path.

Frank stood up and stretched. 'I suppose we had better be going. Have you seen enough?'

Jonathan nodded. 'Thanks for bringing me.'

'I think you would have discovered it for yourself anyway. I'm glad you saw it like this,' said Frank. He raised his hand. 'Listen to that!'

'What?'

'The birds have come back. They make a lovely noise don't they? You know, in a few months the undergrowth will have taken over here again. No one will know anything happened.'

'Some of us will,' said Jonathan.